THE KNIGHTING OF SIR KAYE

map of the knotted woods

Sir Kaye, The Boy Knight® Series Book One

THE KNIGHTING OF SIR KAYE

Don M. Winn
Illustrated by Dave Allred

PUBLISHING

A Cardboard Box Adventures Book

www.donwinn.com

*To Elizabeth, without whom this
book would not have been possible.*

The Knighting of Sir Kaye

ISBN: 978-1-937615-19-2

Copyright © 2012 by Don M. Winn

Published by Cardboard Box Adventures Publishing

www.donwinn.com

The characters and events portrayed in this book are fictitious. Any similarity to real persons, living or dead, is purely coincidental and not intended by the author.

Printed in the United States of America.

Author's Note:

The information I have used to write these stories was first written down by Reginald Stork, royal historian of the kingdom of Knox. When I discovered the records of Sir Kaye's adventures in an ancient and crumbling book from Knox, I thought the stories were so interesting that I wanted to share them with everyone. Therefore, I have changed the language from medieval English to modern English in order to make it easier for people of today to read. I do not think that Reggie would mind. I think he would want everyone to know Kaye's story.

pROLOgue

Long ago, in the days of the knights, good King Frederic of Knox passed away after a grievous illness that lasted for many years. Sadly, when a king becomes sick and slowly worsens over a long period of time, the same thing may happen to the country he rules. And when a good king dies, it may be that a part of his country dies too.

The part of Knox that sickened and died along with the king was called chivalry. Knights are expected to show chivalry, because that is what makes an ordinary knight become a great knight. A chivalrous knight helps other people and shows honor, courage, respect, kindness, and loyalty through his knightly deeds.

But by the time the king died, most of the knights of Knox had already forgotten what chivalry was.

King Frederic left no children to rule after him, and so his young niece Vianne was forced to become the new queen of a country she had never even seen. At nineteen years old, she packed up her things and left her childhood home in the sunny, song-filled country of Vinland. She moved to a new country full of sad-faced strangers and worthless knights who refused to help her make Knox a country to be proud of.

Despite these troubles, Vianne found unexpected help as she tried to rule her difficult kingdom of Knox. One of her first friends was a boy named Kaye, the youngest knight in the history of Knox, and my best friend. My name is Reginald Stork, and this is our story.

CHAPTER ONE

I slammed the door and rushed out into the crooked streets of the city. Usually I watched where I stepped, because the city streets were dirty with garbage and wandering pigs and terrible-smelling puddles, but today I just ran. I dashed through the twisting maze of dark, narrow alleys until I burst through the gate in the city wall and threw myself down to rest in the shade. Taking deep breaths of the fresh air helped me start to calm down.

I had run out of our house that morning with my father's voice thundering in my ears, saying, "I've had enough of you, Reggie. Get out of my sight. Go work in the fields for two weeks with the peasants. Maybe that will make you grateful for the education I'm trying to give you."

At the same time, my mum had called out, "Be careful, Reggie, and watch out for thieves. They'll bump against you and steal your things. You won't know what's happened until it's too late."

I didn't have anything worth stealing, which made me laugh a little. My mum had a funny habit of warning me to be careful about everything, but she didn't bother me.

It was my father who caused all my trouble. He thought I was mad because he was getting me a new tutor, and I let him believe that. I hadn't told him about the real problem—my terrible secret. He would never understand.

My father was a wool merchant in the city of Crofton. He bought wool from farmers and shepherds and other people who owned sheep and then he sold the wool to other merchants in Tellingham, an even larger city by the sea. From there the wool was sold to many other countries. Wool from Knox was famous.

My father loved his job. He planned for me to love it too. As a boy, my father had studied in a monastery with monks, and he was grateful for that education, because it made him a better merchant. Now he was going to give me the finest education from the best tutors and after that he was going to teach me the wool business himself. My future was all planned out for me.

Last week my father decided I needed a second tutor right after he learned that a very important man named Arnold Corson was about to come visit him. Arnold was a very powerful man, the head of the wool merchant's guild in Tellingham. If he liked my father, business was good. If he didn't like my father, business wasn't so good.

My father really wanted Arnold to like him, and he always gave Arnold gifts and tried to impress him with stupid things, like paying two fancy tutors to teach his son.

When I complained about having a new tutor, my father was angry. First he threatened to send me away to learn from the monks. Later he decided that hard work in the fields outside the city would teach me to appreciate the good future and easy life I would have as a wool merchant.

That's why I was now sitting outside the city wall, staring across the fields and thinking about my terrible secret: I hated wool. I never wanted to become a wool merchant.

I liked exploring and collecting things. I liked being where things were happening. I wanted to get away and go somewhere exciting.

The men working in the fields were so far away I could hardly see them. Then I started to grin. That meant that they couldn't see me either. They weren't expecting me. They didn't even know me.

I turned my head to the right. The immense shadows of the Knotted Woods loomed nearby. This gigantic forest stretched across half of Knox. My mum had always warned me that it was full of wild animals and bandits and other dangers. No one had ever told me not to go in there, but I knew that my parents wanted me to stay out of it.

However, I now had two free weeks ahead of me when no one would know where I was, and the Knotted Woods was the perfect place to start exploring. I picked myself up and headed for the edge of the forest.

CHapteR two

The Knotted Woods surprised me. I thought it would be full of dark shadows and wild glowing animal eyes glaring at me through the gloom. I expected pits and traps and snakes and bandits waving knives, but instead, I could hear a stream flowing and birds chirping. Squirrels raced through the tree branches and sunlight fell in patches onto the forest floor. It looked like a friendly place to me.

I decided to start exploring by following the stream so I wouldn't get lost. I followed it for a long time until I came to a clearing in the trees. A long-legged fox sat waiting with his tail wrapped neatly around his feet. He started walking slowly away when he saw me, but then he glanced back at me like he wanted me to follow him. So I did.

That was my first mistake.

The fox started moving faster and faster. Soon I was dodging around tree trunks and jumping over little bushes. Every time I thought I was losing the fox, he'd slow down and let me catch up with him. Then he would speed up again.

We reached another clearing and the fox streaked across it, low to the ground. I was close behind him when he darted under a fallen log, made a sudden sharp turnaround, and dashed back the way we had come. I had already leapt into the air and was sailing over the log. I couldn't change direction in the air, and I landed with both feet right in the middle of one of the Knotted Woods' most deadly traps—quicksand!

I tried pulling my feet out, but that only made me sink faster and deeper into the murky porridge. Then I tried keeping still. That slowed down the sinking a little bit, but I didn't know what else to try. The forest didn't feel very friendly anymore.

I was afraid to shout for help. If the stories about quicksand in the Knotted Woods were true, then the stories about bloodthirsty bandits were true too. I didn't want any bandits to find me here, because I didn't know what they would do to me. However, I knew exactly what the quicksand would do to me. It would suck me down and bury me. I didn't have any choice. I drew in a deep breath, ready to yell for help as loudly as I could, but as I did so, I glanced to the side.

Peering through the bushes was a very interested-looking, ginger-haired, short-nosed, green-eyed boy about my age. My heart almost jumped out of my chest and landed in the quicksand next to me. All my breath came out in a big whuff.

"Hello. You look like you're in over your head," said the boy.

I wasn't sure if I liked his sense of humor.

"Can't you see I need help?" I cried. "Don't make jokes. Please help me."

"Of course I'll help you. Give me a minute and I'll think of something. Don't go anywhere."

I definitely didn't like his sense of humor.

He put his hand on his pointy chin for a second and said, "I'll need a rope of some sort."

Instead of running off to bring back a rope like a normal person, he reached into a small bag he carried and pulled out two short sticks and some gray yarn. He sat cross-legged on the ground and started knitting.

I hoped he was helping me in some way and hadn't just decided to make himself a new pair of socks, but as I watched him I realized he was knitting incredibly fast. It was amazing. Not many people knew how to knit in Knox. Knitting came from the south countries, but I didn't think anyone anywhere could knit like this.

The quicksand was up to my waist now. I put my hands on top of my head to keep them out of the sand. This boy seemed a little crazy, making terrible jokes and sitting at the edge of a pit of quicksand, knitting away as fast as a squirrel climbs a tree. I didn't really trust him to save my life, but I had no choice.

chapter three

"Do you have any brothers or sisters?" the boy asked.

"Um, no," I said. I wasn't in the mood for knitting and pleasant conversation. I didn't want to be polite—I wanted to be rescued.

The boy kept talking. "My sister's named Meg. She's six, and she can't mind her own business. I came here to get away from her. Then I passed Martin's Bog and found you, and I have a feeling that things will go much better for you than they did for old man Martin."

"Old man Martin?" I said, with eyes as wide as a barn owl's eyes.

"Yes. Poor old man Martin died in this bog a long time ago," he said. "That's why it's called Martin's Bog."

"AAAAAAAH! Get me out! Get me out now!" I yelled so loud that I sank another inch deeper in the sand.

"Hold on. I'm almost done. This should do it," he said.

I was stunned to see he had knitted a rope strong enough to pull me out, and just in time. The sand was up to my chest now.

He tied a loop in one end and said, "I don't mean to *knit*-pick, but before I pull you out, maybe you should tell me your name."

"Really? You pick terrible times to make your jokes," I said. "I'm Reggie. Now get me out of here!"

"Nice to meet you, Reggie. My name is Kaye Balfour. Grab the rope and I'll pull you out," he said as he threw me the rope.

I caught it and slid the loop under my arms. "Now pull!" I hollered. With every ounce of his strength, Kaye dragged me out of the sludge and I flopped on the ground at his feet, heaving a big sigh of relief.

"Thanks, Kaye," I said. "I thought I was going to be dinner for worms until you came along. Where did you learn to knit like that?"

Kaye sat down next to me and said, "My grandfather traveled in the south countries a long time ago and learned to knit when he was there. He taught me too, but I don't like to talk about it."

"Why not?" I asked. "You're really fast. And you did save my life with it."

Kaye shrugged. "I want to be a knight like my father. Knights don't knit."

"Who's your father?" I asked. This was exciting. Knights in Knox might be as dangerous as bandits, but they were still knights. They were the famous people who had the adventures that other people only sang songs and told stories about.

"He's Sir Henry Balfour," Kaye said, "and I want to be a knight just like him."

"Sir Henry Balfour," I said. "I can't believe Sir Henry's son saved my life!"

Sir Henry wasn't like the other knights. He was a hero. All the boys wanted to be Sir Henry when we pretended to be knights. He was the best knight that ever lived in Knox, except for Sir Gregory, and Sir Gregory was just in old stories. Sir Henry was real. He had ended a war between Knox and the neighboring country of Eldridge and saved hundreds of lives.

"Where is your father? Can I meet him?" I asked.

Kaye shook his head. "No. He's not here. He's been gone for almost two years." He wouldn't look at me and started throwing twigs into the quicksand.

I didn't know what to say, but I knew Sir Henry wasn't dead. I would have heard about that.

"He didn't just—leave, did he?" I finally asked.

Kaye glared at me. "No! Of course not! The old king sent him away."

My mouth fell open. "He was banished?" That was almost the worst punishment possible. If the king banished you, you had to leave Knox forever. "Was the king mad at him?"

Kaye sighed and said, "No, Reggie. He's working with the king of Eldridge. When the old king of Knox got sick, he needed someone he could trust to help keep the peace between the two kingdoms, so he sent my father to Eldridge."

"Oh," I said. "That makes sense. Don't you miss him?"

I wondered if I would miss my father if he was gone for two years. I guessed I would. Maybe.

"I miss him all the time," Kaye said, "and I miss practicing with him. He was training me to be a knight, and I was going to be his squire."

"Your own father was teaching you?" I asked. That was unusual. Boys who wanted to be knights usually left home and moved in with another knight's family to get their training.

"So what if he was?" Kaye said. "He's a good knight. I learned a lot from him."

I couldn't argue with that, so I asked, "How are you training now that he's gone?"

Kaye looked back down at the ground. "I'm not. He didn't make any other plans for me. So I help my mum at home and wait for him to come back. I hate that. All the boys in the village laugh at me. They say I'll never be a knight because I help my mum and they say I'm too scared to fight because—oh, never mind. It doesn't matter. But you can see why I don't like people to know I can knit."

There was a mystery here, but I didn't ask any more questions. Instead I said, "Well, I won't tell anyone. But with talent like yours, I don't think you can keep it a secret for long."

I needed to leave if I wanted to get home when the field workers finished for the day, but I didn't know where home was.

"Kaye," I said, "do you know how to get to Crofton? I'm lost. I was following a stream, but then I lost that too."

He smiled. "I'll show you how to find it. It's really easy to get lost in these woods. Too bad no one ever made a map of them."

"Wait, Kaye. I have a brilliant idea," I said. "Let's make a map of the woods. We could meet here tomorrow and get started."

"That's perfect! Let's meet here at midmorning. Come on, I'll show you how to get home," Kaye said.

On my way home, I felt excited about the next two weeks. I liked having a new friend to explore with, and I hoped that if Kaye liked me enough, someday I could meet Sir Henry.

When my father saw me, he sniffed at my filthy appearance. "Well, at least you look like you've been working hard. I hope you're beginning to be grateful for the plans I've made for you."

I didn't tell him I had quicksand on me instead of dirt from the fields. He didn't have time to look at me closely, because when my mother saw me she shrieked, pulled me outside, dumped water on me, and started scrubbing.

"Mum," I said as she rubbed at my head, "I met Kaye Balfour today. His father is Sir Henry."

She sloshed another bucket of water over my head and scrubbed at me some more before answering. "So Sir Henry has a son? Well, be nice to that boy. It must be hard to be the son of a famous knight."

"Mum! Of course I'll be nice to him. I want us to be friends."

"I'm glad. Just remember that the best way to have a good friend is to be a good friend," she said as she handed me a towel and went back inside.

I wanted to be a good friend, but I was afraid that wasn't enough. Kaye was a knight's son, and I wasn't sure if I was interesting enough to be his friend. I decided I had to do something about that.

CHAPTER FOUR

It took me a long time to decide what would make Kaye think I was interesting. I thought about it that night as I climbed up to my room in the attic, where I slept and kept my collections. I collected everything. I had sparkling rocks, colored bird feathers, twisted pieces of wood, and anything else I ever found and liked and could carry home. My best treasure was a tiny white frog skeleton with long toes, but I didn't think a knight's son would be very interested in that.

As I was falling asleep, I had an idea. We were about to make a map, and we would need a compass. I just happened to know where to find the most beautiful compass ever made.

My father kept a box in his countinghouse that held his most precious treasures. One of these treasures was a compass. It was a little square glass box with the north-pointing needle carefully balanced inside. Outside, the compass was ornamented with a tiny jeweled dragon curling around the edges of the box. My grandfather the sailor had brought the compass from the south countries, where all the most beautiful things were made. I never knew my grandfather, but I thought I was probably a lot like him.

I wished the compass was mine, but I had heard my father say he was going to give it to Arnold Corson. It made me angry that my father would give away something so beautiful just to impress a stranger and make more money. In two weeks the compass would be gone forever, but in the meantime, I planned to use it for map-making. I hoped Kaye would like it as much as I did.

It was easy to borrow the compass. Early in the morning, I slipped into the empty countinghouse, grabbed the compass, and hid it in a little leather pouch I wore around my neck. Then I ran off to meet Kaye.

That was my second mistake, although I didn't know it at the time.

"Kaye," I called as soon as I saw him, "look what I brought to help us with our map." I pulled the leather pouch over my head and was about to open it, when I realized we were standing in the shadows. "Wait," I said, "come over here into the sun."

I slowly drew the compass out of the pouch and held it so the jewels would sparkle in the sunlight. Kaye's mouth fell open and his eyebrows went up. He took it carefully in his hand and turned it this way and that in the light. The needle spun inside it as he looked at all the sides.

"Reggie, this is wonderful," he said, handing it back to me. "Where did you get it?"

"My grandfather was a sailor. He brought it back from the south countries. And look what else I have," I said as I pulled a little burnt pointed stick and a scrap of parchment out of my shirt. "I can draw a little map with these today, and then I can make a better map on a bigger piece of parchment later."

"You thought of everything, Reggie. I only brought us some dinner," Kaye said.

I almost dropped the compass. "I can't believe I forgot to bring food! I always remember food," I said. "I guess I was too excited about exploring the forest. Good thing you're here."

We decided to map the part of the forest between Kaye's village of Goddard in the east and my city of Crofton in the west. The southern border of our map was the Knox River and an old road called Perilous Trail marked the north edge. Perilous Trail was the only road passing straight through this part of the forest, but it was dangerous because bandits lived along it. Most travelers preferred to use the longer but safer roads that went around the forest.

That morning we found a pit so deep that when we threw rocks and sticks into it, we couldn't hear them hit the bottom. We named it Deadman's Pit, because if you fell in there, you'd be a dead man.

We walked up and down the east side of the forest that day. With every step, the compass pouch brushed against my shirt. I liked knowing it was there, because it made me think of my grandfather.

In the south by the Knox River, Kaye showed me a hidden rock fortress built into a cliff. We couldn't get anywhere near it, but as we watched from far away, we saw lots of men practicing with different types of weapons. They seemed very skillful and very fierce.

Kaye said in a low voice, "That's the fortress of Finsome the Fearsome, one of the most dangerous bandits in Knox. We shouldn't go anywhere near it. We shouldn't even know it exists. Come on, let's get away from here."

We were creeping quietly away when I banged my knee against something half-buried in the leaf mulch that covered the forest floor. It hurt, but it didn't feel like a stone or a tree root.

"Wait, Kaye, I found something," I whispered. It was hard and pointed and made of metal. I pulled on it and dug around it and found out it was much bigger than I had first thought.

"Here," Kaye said. He handed me a stick for digging and found one for himself. Together we crouched on the ground and dug carefully around the object.

"What do you think it is?" I said softly.

"I don't know," he said. "Maybe a piece of armor?"

That got me excited. "It will be the best thing in my collection," I said a little too loudly.

"Shhh. Don't let them hear you. The people in that fortress are dangerous."

I nodded and we dug faster, scraping the earth out from around the thing. It was starting to look round. "I think it's a helmet," I whispered.

"Find the front and pull it out," Kaye said.

I dug my fingers into the open part in the front of the helmet and pulled. The helmet started to loosen from the ground. With one more tug, it came free. The inside was packed full of dirt, but that didn't matter to me.

"I got it!" I cried. Half a second later, an arrow thudded into one of the nearby trees just over our heads.

"They heard us!" Kaye whispered. "Hurry! We have to get away from here! We can't let them find us!"

In an instant, he swept his arm across the ground and filled the hole we had made with leaves and things from the forest floor. We started crawling away as fast as we could. I tried to be quiet as I scurried along, holding the helmet awkwardly under my arm.

Two more arrows went singing through the air and disappeared over our heads somewhere. I saw a third arrow land right in front of me. Even though we were running for our lives, I had to grab it as we passed. I could hear distant shouts from behind us, near the river.

chapter five

When the shouts grew fainter, Kaye paused and listened carefully to the peaceful forest noises.

"I think we might be safe now," he said. "At least we can stand up and run."

We ran north, according to my compass readings, and then kept on exploring, but as we came to a certain part of the forest near Kaye's village, he wouldn't let me go anywhere near it.

"We can't go in there," he said.

"Why not?" I asked. "We're explorers. We need to explore. We already escaped bandits. What could be worse than that?"

"We just can't go in there. I promised that I wouldn't," he replied.

"Who made you promise that?" I asked.

"Charles. Charles Atwood," he said. "It's his secret hideout. I found him there one time and he was furious. I promised I would never go back there."

"Who's Charles Atwood?" I asked.

Kaye was slow to answer. "He's a boy from my village. He's, um, really big. We used to be best friends, but now he hates me and I don't know why. I never did anything to him—at least I don't think I did."

I didn't like the sound of this. Maybe Kaye wished that he was exploring with Charles instead of with me. I kicked at a stone. "Well, if he hates you, I don't see why you have to keep a promise to him," I finally said. "I think we should go in there anyway."

Kaye stopped walking and pulled my arm to stop me too. The compass pouch bumped against my chest as I stopped.

Kaye made me look at him and said, "I made a promise, Reggie. I want to keep it. That's what my father taught me, so I'm going to do it even if Charles does hate me."

I made a face at this, but I could tell I wasn't going to be able to change his mind. He listened to everything his father said. My father would be so happy if I did that. But the difference between us was that Kaye wanted to be like his father. I didn't.

"Fine," I said. "I'll put a skull and crossbones on that part of the map."

"Good idea," Kaye said as we kept walking.

I still was curious about the friendship between Kaye and Charles. "Kaye," I said, "how do you know Charles hates you?"

He sighed. "Trust me. I know."

"Tell me about it," I said.

He started speaking slowly. "Well, all of the boys in the village used to play together. Our favorite game was to have jousting tournaments. We didn't have horses of course, but we used to run at each other and try to knock each other down. The winner was the one left standing. Charles and I and a boy named Peter were always the best."

I nodded. I had played games like this with the town boys.

Kaye kept talking. "One day we had an extra good tournament planned. We even made two tents for putting on our pretend armor. I was excited that day. My father had just started my training and everyone knew it. I felt like I had a real chance at winning that day. I was going to joust with Peter. Just before I came out of the tent, Charles threw water over my pants."

"Why?" I asked.

"Well, he pushed me outside and told everyone I had wet my pants because I was too scared to fight Peter. They all laughed at me and now everyone believes it's true. They think I'll never be a real knight. Sometimes I wonder if they're right. Now none of the other boys want to have anything to do with me. They all like Charles best."

His voice was hard and bitter, like wild green raspberries. I felt happier because now I knew I could be a better friend than Charles, but at the same time I felt bad that Kaye had lost his friends.

"Do you think Charles was jealous that you were being trained by your father? Maybe he was worried that you would be a lot better than him and Peter that day," I said.

Kaye looked thoughtful. "No. Charles never cared about being a knight. He always wanted to work at the same thing his father did."

I could not believe this. I dropped the helmet and arrow I was carrying to the ground and crossed my arms over the leather pouch. "Why do all the boys in your village want to do exactly what their fathers do? I don't want to do what my father does. It's so boring. It's all wool all day long and it's always the same. I want to travel and explore and collect things that aren't wool!" I cried.

Kaye laughed. "I don't want to work with wool either. Do you know that my grandfather wants me to knit and teach others and start a workshop and sell knitted clothes? He says I could make a fortune with my talent and make Knox famous. But that's not what I want to do."

I laughed too. "Well I can understand that, but my father would go mad with excitement to see you knit. He could make money off your knitting for sure."

We were standing on top of a tiny hill near Charles' hide-out. I glanced up at the sun and realized it was time to go home, so I pulled out the compass and checked my directions so I could find my stream again. Once I was sure of the right direction, I put it carefully in the pouch, closed it tightly, and put it back around my neck. Then I picked up the helmet and the arrow.

"See you tomorrow, Kaye?" I asked.

"Yes. Let's meet at midday by Deadman's Pit," he said.

"Good. I'll see you then," I said. We both jumped down from the hill at the same time and bumped against each other. "Sorry," I called. "See you tomorrow."

I was soon heading home. I was glad to have a friend I could explore with who understood how terribly boring wool was to me. I was so excited to have a real knight's helmet *and* a real bandit's arrow to add to my collection that I went leaping along through the woods.

When I came to a small cliff where the stream fell down in a waterfall, I decided to jump it. I reached the edge and leapt out into the air and landed with a thump, feeling free and happy as I headed home.

Much later, I slipped into the countinghouse to return the compass and realized it was gone. My bones and my insides turned to water and I felt like I needed to either sit down or fall down.

This was terrible. My father would be furious. He had already promised Arnold the compass. Now he would have to tell Arnold I had lost it and Arnold would hate me and my father. Then my father would be even more angry with me. He would send me off to live with the monks. Then I'd never get to do any more exploring. Life would just be study, study, study, and then wool, wool, wool.

I didn't know what I would do.

chapter six

I couldn't sleep that night. I thought and thought about where the compass could have fallen off my neck. I remembered using it near Charles' hideout to figure out where to find my stream. I also remembered that when I leapt off the tiny cliff by the waterfall, I hadn't felt the leather bag bump against my chest. It must have disappeared before that.

I really hoped it hadn't fallen into the stream. Maybe it was lying on the forest floor, waiting for me to find it. Maybe it would only take a few minutes of searching to find it. Maybe everything would be fine and I wouldn't have to go live with the monks.

Early the next morning, I carefully searched every inch of the forest floor between the waterfall and Charles' hideout. I couldn't find it, so I stood on the tiny hill near the hideout and turned slowly around, wondering what to do next. When I faced the hideout again, I jumped off the hill and suddenly remembered bumping against Kaye yesterday in the same spot. I also remembered one of my mum's warnings about thieves that steal things when bumping into people.

That's when I started to wonder if Kaye had stolen my compass. He thought it was very beautiful. Did he think it was beautiful enough to steal it from me?

I started to get angry as I thought about it. How dare he take something that was mine, something that was so important to me? I was staring at Charles' hideout at that moment, and I was angry enough that I decided to do what Kaye wouldn't let me do yesterday: I decided to go inside and finish exploring.

I entered a circle of low-branched pines around a small clearing. Tall oak trees grew across from me and there were good boulders for climbing under the trees.

On the west side of the clearing was a big pile of sticks that looked like a beaver dam. It had a door, so I suppose it was a kind of hut, but it was the worst-looking hut I had ever seen. It looked like it had been built by a blind beaver with broken teeth.

I walked over to the beaver hut and gently pulled open the door. I didn't want anything to fall apart. It was empty except for a rough wooden box in the middle of the space with some cuts in the top. I lifted the top off the box and looked inside. I saw two crooked wooden cups and two lop-sided wooden bowls.

Then I saw a perfect wooden carving of a wolf gazing off into the distance. Its ears were pricked and so alert that I found myself trying to listen for whatever sound it had heard. It looked like it was about to take off running. Underneath it I found two really bad wooden wolves and a clumsy carving of a girl. I only knew it was supposed to be a girl because of the skirts. It seemed like the blind beaver had decided to chew himself some wood art. There wasn't much else to see, so I closed everything and left the clearing.

I wondered if I should tell Kaye about the beaver hut and the carvings.

Part of me thought there might be a helpful clue there about why Charles now hated Kaye. The other part of me was still mad at Kaye and didn't want to help him. I hated the idea that Kaye might have taken my compass, so I had to go find out the truth.

I decided to go find Kaye at home.

chapter seven

I stepped out of the forest and saw a castle and the village of Goddard in the middle of fields of rye and barley and pastures full of sheep. Goddard wasn't a big village, but it had an inn, a barber-surgeon, and some merchant stalls where you could buy just about anything you could want—it was almost as good as a fair that way. I saw bright silks that caught the light like colored glass windows and I smelled spices that must have come from far-away countries.

Most of the houses were very small, with chickens wandering in and out of them, but others looked like they might have two rooms and even an attic loft. I hoped Kaye lived in the castle, although he had never mentioned it. If I lived in a castle, I'd want to tell people about it!

As I looked around, I accidentally backed right into a big boy, knocking him over into a pile of sheep dung.

"Look at what you did, you lummox!" the boy yelled. "Why don't you watch where you're going?"

"Oh, I'm sorry," I said. "I was just looking for Sir Henry Balfour's house."

He pointed at the castle. "It's behind you, you idiot!" He picked up a big handful of dung and threw it right at me, spattering my shirt with the dusty pellets. Before he could throw any more insults or dung at me I quickly ran off toward the castle.

I did feel like an idiot, especially with my shirt so befouled. I brushed it off the best I could—at least it wasn't fresh manure—and I made my way to the castle gates.

They were standing wide open and people went freely in and out. I walked through the entrance and came into the big sunny courtyard of the castle, where I stopped and stared. It was like there was an entire village inside the walls.

I saw a man shoeing a horse and another man repairing some armor next to the biggest stables I had ever seen. There was a pigsty and a garden where I saw leeks, onions, peas, beans, and other vegetables growing. There was even an orchard inside the walls. Chickens and geese were wandering around, pecking at the dirt and getting in everyone's way. I saw a cattle shed and the dairy next to it. A few little children waited outside the open doorway of a small stone building until the baker came out and handed them each a piece of bread, hot from the oven. I liked this castle!

I wandered inside and had almost crossed the whole courtyard when I realized I didn't know where to go. Then a really good smell drifted across my way and said hello to my nose, which made my stomach so jealous that it growled. If I could trust my nose—and I can always trust my nose—I had found the kitchens, which had to be near the great hall where everyone ate together at mealtimes. Sooner or later, Kaye would come there too, so that's where I decided to look for him.

I had just turned toward the hall when I almost fell over a little girl running straight at me. She didn't stop until there was only a handbreadth of air left between us. She stared at me harder than a hunting hawk.

Her face and clothes were streaked and dusty, like she had been rubbing ashes on herself, and her dark red hair flew every which way with more ashes in it. The only clean things about her were her bright blue eyes. This had to be Kaye's sister Meg.

"Who are you? What are you doing here?" she asked.

I didn't like the way she talked to me. "I'm Reggie and I'm here to see Kaye."

"Why do you want to see Kaye?" Meg demanded. Right about then, Kaye and his mum appeared behind Meg.

"This is Reggie and he wants to see Kaye," Meg said, "but he didn't say why."

"That's fine, Meg. Don't crowd the boy," Kaye's mum said.

Meg took a small step back and said, "I don't know where he came from, but I think he's come a long way. He's dirty."

I blushed. I thought I had gotten all the sheep dung off me. I guess I had missed some.

Kaye laughed. "Meg, you're filthy yourself. Hello, Reggie, it's good to see you."

I was glad Kaye was happy to have me visit, but I also felt bad because I really only came to get my compass back.

Kaye's mum finally noticed how dirty Meg was and she didn't think it was anything to laugh about. "Meg, this is shameful! What have you been into?"

"Nothing. Just the kitchens. I was helping with the meat pies. But I fell in the flour. Then the cook wouldn't let me help anymore, so I was watching the birds on the spits and

I fell into the hearth. Then Cook was mad and said I got ashes in the custard but I didn't see any and when I told him that, he said I was never allowed in the kitchens again. Please make him let me go back, Mum? Please?"

"We'll talk about that after you're clean," she said. Then she turned to me, "Welcome to our home, Reggie. How do you two know each other?" she asked Kaye much more politely than Meg would have.

"Oh," Kaye said, "we met the other day while I was out walking. Reggie, this is my mum, Lady Martha."

"I see," Lady Martha said. "Well, welcome Reggie, I'm happy to meet any friend of Kaye's."

"That's because he doesn't have any!" Meg shrieked. Now Kaye turned red.

I had to do something. I put my hand on my chest and made a deep bow like the minstrels do in the marketplace when they finish their stories. "Thank you, Lady Martha. It's an honor to make your acquaintance," I said.

Lady Martha smiled, and even Meg looked impressed. Then Lady Martha said, "Reggie, we will be eating soon, and if you have traveled a long way, you must be hungry. I hope that you will join us for dinner."

"We're having meat pie and I helped make it," Meg said.

"I would like that, Lady Martha, thank you again." I said.

"I'm going to show Reggie around," Kaye said, and he quickly whisked me off to the stable, with Meg following close behind.

The stable was magnificent. It was at least twenty feet tall and had stalls for up to twenty horses, although only six of them were filled. Kaye took me over to introduce me to his horse. He stopped in front of the biggest horse I had ever seen. He was a lovely dark gray color with a white streak down his forehead and his eyes made him look smarter than some people I have met.

"Reggie, this is my horse, Kadar!" Kaye said proudly. "My father gave him to me when he first taught me how to ride. I was only eight. I remember how big Kadar seemed to me back then."

"Back then!" I yelled. "He's still enormous. And you learned to ride on him? He's too big for an eight-year-old to ride. He's even too big for a twelve-year-old to ride. That's a war horse!"

chapter eight

Kadar lowered his head at the sound of my voice and began sniffing at my hair like he was a very tall dog. I wanted to run away, but it felt funny, like he was trying to get to know me, so I stood still. Then I had the strange idea that Kadar was trying to make me be quiet. I guess it worked, because I wasn't yelling anymore. I felt calmer than I had felt since I discovered the compass was missing.

I reached up to pat his nose and he let me. Then I asked Kaye, "What does he think of me?"

Kaye had been watching with a very interested expression on his face. "I think he likes you, Reggie. He's a smart horse, and he knows people."

I stared at Kadar even harder. "What would happen if he didn't like me?"

Kaye shrugged. "I don't know for sure, but you probably would have run out of the stable a long time ago. He has big scary hooves when he rears up and starts waving them around your head."

Kadar bent his gigantic head and rubbed it lovingly against Kaye's chest, and Kaye laughed. "Kadar is really a very kind horse. He's always been gentle with me. He's even gentle with Meg, and she annoys him sometimes."

"I do not," Meg said, getting all ruffled up like a chicken coming in from the rain. One glance from Kadar quieted her down again. He let her give him a dried-up apple from last autumn's harvest, which he seemed to enjoy more than I would have.

Kaye kept talking. "I told you my father taught me to ride, but Kadar did too. He's had a lot of training—he really is a warhorse, just like you said, and he knows what makes a good rider."

"Why did you name him Kadar?" I asked.

He shrugged. "I didn't. That was already his name. It's a name from another country. I think it might be where he was born. Kadar means strong, and he is very strong."

Meg pulled on my arm. "My horse is named Kadar too," she said, and I heard Kaye heave a sigh behind me as she tugged me toward another stall. In it was a delicate chestnut mare, whose coat matched Meg's hair perfectly. Of course, the horse was cleaner than Meg.

Meg found another one of those withered apples and pushed it into my hand. "Don't be afraid, you can feed it to her," she encouraged me, patting me on the arm and acting like I was much younger than she was.

I frowned. "I'm not afraid of horses! I know how to ride."

Meg grinned at me like she enjoyed making me get up-in-arms about something. "You were afraid of Kaye's Kadar when you first saw him," she said.

I narrowed my eyes at her. "I was impressed, not afraid. Why did you name your horse the same as Kaye's horse? That's strange." Kadar the Second pulled the apple off of my hand and was calmly chewing it.

Now she was upset. "It is not strange! My Kadar is strong too!"

Kaye stepped between us. "Yes, she is, Meg. And she likes Reggie too. Let's go eat now. I'm hungry for your meat pies."

Meg was distracted by this and ran ahead of us to the great hall with a big smile. Kaye was a lot like his horse. He could make people calm down almost as well as Kadar the First. He just wasn't as big.

As we left the stables, Kaye whispered to me, "Mum named Meg's horse Cider, because of its color. Meg just thinks it's the same as Kadar."

"Kaye, wait," I said as soon as Meg was gone. "I have to tell you something terrible. I lost the compass yesterday. I searched the woods this morning, but it's gone." I felt like I was going to cry, but of course I didn't. Instead I watched Kaye carefully, to see if he looked guilty. He didn't. He just looked upset.

"I'll help you, Reggie. We'll go look for it again tomorrow morning. Meet me at Deadman's Pit as early as you can. Maybe it was under some leaves and you just missed it this morning. I'm sure it's there," he said.

I shook my head slowly. "I looked really hard, Kaye. I don't know what I'm going to do. It's my father's compass. When he finds out I lost it, he'll be so mad he'll send me to school with the monks, I just know it. He's supposed to give the compass to a really important man who's coming to visit in two weeks."

Kaye thumped my shoulder and said, "We'll find it, Reggie. We have two weeks. A lot can happen in two weeks."

I felt a little better. Maybe Kaye hadn't taken my compass. Maybe we could still be friends. I still had one more thing to tell him though.

"Kaye, I explored Charles Atwood's hideout in the forest this morning," I said.

"What? Reggie, I promised I wouldn't do that."

"Well you didn't do it. I did. He's got an awful little beaver hut in there and inside he has carvings. There's a beautiful wolf, and two really awful ones. And," I said, starting to laugh, "there's a really bad carving of a girl or something. It's like an ugly doll. That's probably why he made you stay away. He didn't want anyone to find out he goes off to the woods to play with dolls!"

Kaye snorted as he laughed out loud. "No wonder he was so mad when I found his hideout!" As soon as we calmed down, Kaye looked thoughtful and said, "I bet he's just out there practicing wood carving. His father used to be an amazing wood-carver and probably made the good wolf. Charles might be trying to copy his father's things. Reggie—what's a beaver hut?"

"It's a hut that looks like a big old pile of sticks—like a beaver dam, of course," I said. "But wait a minute. Why did you say Charles' father used to be a wood carver? Is he dead?"

Kaye shook his head. "I don't think so. He left. About two years ago he took his extra shirt and all the food in the house and never came back. So now it's just Charles and his mother."

"Oh. Well maybe he hates you because his father left."

"I thought of that," Kaye said, "but it doesn't make sense. I didn't make his father leave. Even Charles would know that. It's no reason for him to hate me."

"Well, maybe—" I began, but my stomach interrupted with a hungry noise.

"Maybe we should just go eat," Kaye said.

I thought that was a good idea.

When we entered the hall, we washed our hands at a large stone basin just inside the door. As I was drying my hands, Kaye nudged me and pointed to a wonderful carving of an enormous stag above the fireplace. Its antlers branched out like a tree and its legs looked strong enough to jump over the crowded room.

"Charles' father made that," whispered Kaye as he led me to the family table at the head of the room. Meg looked much better after washing up, although she seemed more than a little damp.

There was an older man there too—probably Kaye's grandfather. He had dark rough hair and a dark rough beard that were both streaked with gray. He wore an eye patch over one eye. He didn't say much but he looked at me sharply with his good eye. Then Kaye and I were each served some meat pie and I forgot about everything else. After my first bite, I couldn't stop eating.

"This is the best meat pie I've ever eaten!" I said to Lady Martha, "And I've eaten a lot of meat pies."

"Why, thank you, Reggie. Would you like some more?"

"Yes, please," I said. Then I devoured the second helping. I wanted to ask for a third helping too, but I was starting to get embarrassed, so I didn't.

"Mum, can Reggie and I go riding after dinner?" Kaye asked.

"That will be fine, Kaye," Lady Martha said.

"And I'm going too," Meg said, as though that was just the way it was going to be.

"Maybe another time," Kaye said. "Today is your day for a knitting lesson with Grandfather."

Meg scrunched up her face like she was getting ready to squeal, but she was stopped short by Kaye's grandfather.

"Margaret, enough! Today you will knit. Get your things and bring them to our rooms. Kaye, ride in the direction of the sheep shearing and watch to see that they are using enough soap. I do not care for dirty wool. Speak to John Temple if you think they need more washing." His voice was dark and rough like his beard.

"Yes, Grandfather Wulfric," they both answered. Meg ran meekly off to do what he said.

As Kaye's grandfather passed us on his way to the family rooms, he looked straight at me and briefly closed his eye. I jumped a little in my chair. Was he trying to wink at me?

Kaye loaned me a horse named Parsnip. We were about to leave the castle and head through the village when Kaye spoke up, saying, "If you want to see Charles, he'll probably find us in the village. He always tries to tease me until I'm angry. It takes all of my strength to ignore him."

In the short time that I'd known Kaye, I'd noticed that nothing seemed to bother him, not quicksand or bandits or a sister that was as irritating as a flea bite or anything else—only Charles Atwood.

"Ignore him?" I said. "Your father taught you how to fight, didn't he? Why don't you just teach old Charles a lesson he'll never forget? I bet he won't tease you after that!"

"That's not what my father taught me," Kaye said. "He taught me to use my brains to solve problems. He said it takes more strength *not* to fight, especially when someone is trying to make trouble. Besides, there's a part of me that still thinks of Charles as my friend and—I don't know—I guess I just don't want to fight him."

"Hmmph," I said. "Well you have more patience than I do if you keep letting him tease you." I was about to find out that I was wrong about that.

CHAPTER NINE

As soon as we passed through the gates, a big boy came running into view. He slowed down when he saw the two of us together and smiled a mean smile. Then he headed straight toward us.

"That's him," Kaye said in a low voice.

Of course it was. It was the sheep-dung boy. I should have known. If anyone was going to be throwing sheep dung around, it was Charles Atwood.

Charles was twelve years old like Kaye and me, but he was huge. He looked like he was sixteen. His clothes looked like they had belonged to his grandfather and I would have been surprised if he had even washed his face once in the past three months. Of course I had knocked him into a pile of sheep manure earlier that day. That probably didn't make him look any cleaner.

"Well, well, if it isn't little Kaye Balfour and his friend the dung beetle!" Charles said. "Shouldn't you be doing housework with your mummy and the women servants? Who's the dung beetle you have with you? Is it your new nurse?"

I blushed. I hadn't told Kaye about my earlier meeting with Charles. I thought for sure Kaye would do something, but he just ignored Charles.

"Come on, Reggie," Kaye said, "we need to get down to the river."

I leaned over to Kaye and whispered, "Kaye, aren't you going to say something? You can't just let that go."

"Yes, I can," Kaye muttered back, "and so can you." His face had no expression on it.

I should have just kept still, but Charles had already noticed that I was bothered by his words. He trailed after us as we made our way through the village and his bullying kept getting louder. People gathered around to watch—mostly other boys.

"Are you deaf, Kaye?" Charles said, "Or just stupid? I asked if that was your nurse with you! He looks to be even weaker than you are. Does he want to be a knight too? Is he training with the ladies the same way you are, Sir Spindle? Sir Dairy Maid? Sir Wet-nurse?"

Kaye turned bright red and his jaw bulged from how hard he was clenching it. His hands gripping the reins were white.

I couldn't take it anymore. "Kaye, aren't you going to say something?" I whispered. I couldn't believe that Kaye could just ignore Charles.

One of the boys watching tossed a piece of half-chewed bread at Kaye's head. I glanced at Kaye and he was staring down at Kadar's neck looking blotchy-faced and completely miserable.

Some of the other boys were sniggering. This inspired Charles to make one last great effort. "You there, Nurse, if you're going to look after Kaye, I hope you've brought plenty of swaddling. He still wets himself when he's scared, you know! Kaye, it's no wonder your father gave up on trying to make you into a knight and left the country!"

All the sniggering boys standing around burst out laughing long and loud.

Suddenly Kaye slid off Kadar, picked up a big handful of wet, sloppy mud and threw it directly at Charles, smacking him right on the forehead. "What do you know about it, Charles?" Kaye yelled. "You're the one who goes off to the forest to play with wooden dogs and dolls!"

Charles stared at Kaye with a shocked and hurt expression on his face, but the shock turned to fury in an instant. "Those were my FATHER'S!" he screamed. "You're going to get the beating of your life when I get my hands on you!"

Kaye's eyes were as big as boiled eggs as he stood there staring at Charles with his mouth open. He was so surprised at what he had done that he couldn't move. Charles was rushing toward him, so I reached down, grabbed Kaye's shoulder, and shoved him toward his horse.

"Get on your horse, Kaye!" I yelled. "Be quick about it!"

That was just what he needed to get moving. One moment later he was safe on Kadar and we were making our way quickly out of the village.

As soon as we were clear of the village, Kaye and Kadar took off across the pastures, galloping faster than a rainstorm comes when there's nowhere to hide from it.

I tried to follow them, but Parsnip was no match for Kadar. So I headed for the top of the last hill I had seen them climb. From there, I saw Kaye and Kadar down among the willow trees by the river. Further downstream and past the castle I saw men standing in the river washing the sheep to get them ready for shearing.

I rode down to Kaye. He was sitting on the ground in front of Kadar, and Kadar was snuffling at his hair. I climbed off of Parsnip and sat near Kaye. We looked at the water for a while. Kaye was still red and blotchy, but he looked calmer.

Finally he broke the silence. "I really shouldn't have done that," he said.

"Well, he deserved it," I said. "He was being awful to you."

Kaye shook his head. "No. I was wrong to do it. My father would be so disappointed in me. A good knight helps people. He doesn't make things worse."

"Kaye, you're not thinking straight. If your father had been there he probably would have dunked Charles in the river a few times until he cooled down and stopped being so mean."

"Did you see his face?" Kaye asked. "I knew those things you found in his beaver hut had something to do with his father. I knew it would hurt his feelings if I said anything about them, but I did it anyway."

"What made you do it?" I asked. "You ignored everything he said, and then suddenly you were throwing mud and yelling at him. What happened?"

Kaye shrugged. "It was because he said my father gave up on training me. Sometimes I wonder if that's true. He wouldn't let me go train with another family like all the other boys who want to be knights. Maybe I'm no good. Maybe I'll never be a knight. Maybe he's just waiting until I'm older to tell me that I shouldn't be a knight."

I shook my head. "Kaye, don't be foolish. Your father never planned to leave the country. That had nothing to do with you. He's doing a good thing for you by teaching you himself. I'm sure of that. I trust him. Don't you?"

Kaye looked confused. "Yes, I trust him."

"Then don't give up. Nobody tells stories about knights that are exactly like everybody else. Your father is the best knight in the land, and he's teaching you to be a knight in the way that's right for you."

Kaye looked at me like this was a whole new idea. I was getting nervous, because he was staring at me so hard. So I started talking again.

"Kaye, I didn't tell you, but Charles threw sheep manure at me before I came to your house today. That's why I was so dirty."

He started to smile. "Why didn't you tell me?"

"Because I felt like a fool—a smelly fool," I answered.

"You're not a fool, Reggie," Kaye said. After a few seconds he added, "You are kind of smelly, though."

I pushed him over and Kadar stuck his face between us and *whooshed* his breath at me. I think he was giving me a stern look.

"Fine, fine, Kadar. I'll leave him alone," I said.

"Yes, you had better leave me alone," Kaye said. "Kadar is a serious horse. He won't permit any kind of *horse*-play when he's around." That awful joke pleased him so much that he laid back on the ground and laughed a little too hard.

I didn't think his joke was quite that funny. So I smiled like I do when I have stomach pains and my mother tells me how brave I am to swallow her bitter medicines of mint and wormwood.

When Kaye finished laughing at himself and sat up, I said to him, "Kaye, do you want to know something else funny? Today I came to your house to see if maybe you had taken the compass. I was so worried when I couldn't find it this morning that I remembered how we bumped into each other in the forest yesterday. I thought maybe you grabbed it when I wasn't paying attention." I meant to tell him this so we could laugh about it, but it didn't happen that way.

Instead, everything changed in an instant. Kaye jumped to his feet and said coldly, "You thought I was a thief? How could you? Maybe I lost my temper today, but that was an accident. I'm *not* a thief. I think you should go home, Reggie."

Kaye got back onto Kadar and took off in the direction of the castle. They were soon out of sight. I didn't really have any choice but to follow after him. When I got there, I took Parsnip back to the stables and a groom took care of him, but Kadar and Kaye were nowhere to be seen. I decided I might as well start the long walk home.

I wondered if Kaye would meet me tomorrow as we had planned or if I had lost my new friend for good.

chapter ten

The next morning I woke up early. I had to go to the forest to search for the compass, but I didn't know if I should bother trying to meet Kaye. I had a feeling he wouldn't be waiting for me.

Maybe my mum could help. I found her in the kitchen, putting some food in a pouch for me. I thought she hadn't noticed when I forgot my dinner a few days ago, but she had. Ever since then, she made sure I didn't leave without it.

"Mum?" I asked.

"Here's your dinner, Reggie. Leave it in the shade until you eat so the sun doesn't spoil it," she said. Then she looked over at me. "What's wrong, Reggie?"

"Mum, did you ever have a friend get really mad at you?" I asked.

"Of course, Reggie. That's happened to everyone. What's wrong? Did you and Kaye have a fight?" she asked.

"No. I don't think we did. But I said something he didn't like and now he's mad at me. I wasn't trying to make him mad. I didn't know it would bother him. I think he was wrong to act like he did," I said.

My mum came over to me and put her arm around me. "Reggie, people are the most important part of life. Don't let yourself lose a friend just because of some small mistakes. Go find your friend and figure things out."

I nodded my head. "I think—I think I was going to do that anyway, Mum. Thanks. And thanks for the dinner," I said as I went out the door. I felt bad letting my mum think I was going off to work in the fields, especially after she had just been so nice to me. I wanted to tell her the truth, but I just had to find that compass first.

I went straight to Deadman's Pit. If Kaye came there, he would find me waiting. If he didn't come by midday, I would go find him. If I didn't try to find him, that would have been my third and worst mistake, and I had already made enough mistakes that week.

I had only waited a few minutes—which I spent throwing pinecones into the pit—when I heard someone coming through the woods. I hid behind a nearby rock in case it was Charles, but it wasn't. It was Kaye.

He looked around as he got close to the pit, but when he didn't see anything or anyone, his face fell. He sat down with his back against a tree like he was planning to wait a while.

I came out from behind the rock. "Kaye?" I called.

He looked up and his face relaxed when he saw me. "Reggie!" he cried. "I hoped you would be here."

I nodded. "I hoped you would be here too. Listen, Kaye, I'm sorry I thought you might have taken the compass. I was just trying to think of any place it could be. I was really upset I lost it."

"I know," Kaye said. "I shouldn't have gotten so mad. I was still upset about Charles. I came here really early this morning to wait for you. When you didn't come, I gave up and went home, but I came back again."

"Why did you come back?" I asked.

"I didn't want to lose my best friend."

"Really?" I cried. "Better than Charles?"

He nodded. "I have to help you find the compass anyway. I don't want you to have to go study with the monks. Then I would never see you again."

I shivered at the thought of the dusty monks in their cold monastery with their endless books. "Let's start looking for it now!" I said.

So we searched every inch of the ground between Charles' hideout and the little waterfall. We didn't find anything. I sank down in a pile of dead leaves under a tree, closed my eyes, put my head in my hands, and groaned.

"Kaye, it's no good. It's gone. I'll never find it. I'll have to go live with the monks."

Kaye sat down next to me and opened the little bag he always wore at his side. "Would some dinner help?" he asked.

"No," I groaned again. "I'll never be hungry again."

"Are you sure? I brought some extra meat pie from yesterday," he said.

I peeked out from between my fingers. "Meat pie?"

Kaye waved it under my nose. The smell made my mouth cry. I gave in.

"I guess I'll still have to eat," I said as I started on the pie.

"That's the spirit," Kaye said. "Don't give up. We still have almost two weeks, and we'll look again after we finish eating."

I shook my head. "No, Kaye, it's useless. I probably dropped it in the stream. Let's just keep exploring and finish our map. We haven't explored the south or the west side of the forest. Let's do that today."

Kaye looked concerned. "Are you sure, Reggie? We don't have to give up yet."

"I'm sure," I said.

"Well," Kaye said, "maybe a bird or something carried it off to another part of the forest. Maybe we'll find it while we're exploring."

I shook my head again and said, "That's impossible, Kaye. Thanks for trying. Let's go down to the river and follow it west today."

That's what we did, and that's where we found the treasure caves. They weren't filled with gold and gems, but they held their own kinds of treasures.

In the high riverbank near the western edge of the forest, there was a honeycomb of shallow caves. People had camped here before and left things behind, like an old rusted cooking pot and tattered pieces of cloth. I found marks of old cooking fires in some of the higher caves.

The lower caves flooded whenever the river rose. They were full of mud and forest trash, but we also found treasures the river had washed into the caves. I found a broken birdcage made of little sticks tied together. Kaye found an old fishing net.

"Reggie, let's keep this net. I think we could use it for catching rabbits!" he said.

I examined the net. "Aren't there too many holes in it? The rabbits will get out again."

He shook his head and said, "No, I can fix them with knitting. It will be perfect."

We dragged the net out of the muddy cave and dunked it in the river until the mud was gone. I hoped we would catch a fish, but even though we tried for a while, it didn't happen, so we spread the net out to dry.

When we went home that evening, Kaye ran off with his net, saying, "I'll meet you here early tomorrow, and don't worry, Reggie, we're going to find the compass soon. Maybe even tomorrow!"

"Kaye, you're being ridiculous," I called after him. "It's impossible!"

"I can't HEAR you," he yelled from the distance.

It was strange that this time Kaye was so much more optimistic than I was. It was crazy to think that we would find it tomorrow, but I couldn't help hoping he was right.

chapter eleven

A gray fog crept in during the night and stayed all the next day. Everything was quiet and even though I was awake, I felt like I was dreaming. Kaye and I met at the treasure caves and continued exploring without finding much.

Just before dinnertime, we heard a strange noise. It sounded like a wild animal growling and huffing to itself. It sounded like a hungry noise to me.

I glanced at Kaye and he nodded, so we tiptoed closer, as quietly as possible. Near the edge of a clearing, we paused and peered through the trees. Then we grinned at each other. It was nothing more than some men, lying around the clearing and snoring and snorting away. Two of them were awake—one was stirring a pot over the fire and the other one was leaning against a tree with his long legs propped up on a big rock. Sitting that way, he looked like the letter V, and he was whittling at a stick with his knife. The ground around him was covered with wood shavings.

Kaye nudged me in the ribs with his elbow and then pointed upward. We were standing under a tree with large, sturdy branches, and I could tell he wanted us to climb the tree and spy on them, but I didn't see how four sleeping men, a whittler, and a stew-stirrer could be worth watching.

Kaye poked me harder and raised his eyebrows. I shrugged and let him climb up first. He had his fishnet looped around his waist and one shoulder, but I didn't know why. There were no rabbits to capture up in that tree. I was sure he had spent last night mending the holes in the net so it would be ready for rabbits. I was starting to notice that when Kaye got an idea in his head, it stayed there.

I climbed up after him and we perched on a branch like tired birds, hidden in the leaves and the fog. After waiting a little while for nothing to happen, I jabbed Kaye with my finger and pointed down. He shook his head and pointed to the clearing, so I studied it, trying to see what he found so interesting. One of the sleeping men had bright red hair. The stew-stirring man, who was short and wore a faded red hood and scarf, salted his stew once or twice. Nothing else happened.

Then the whittling man stood up and stuck his knife back into his belt next to a wooden flute. He stretched his arms above his head and a thousand little shreds of wood fell to the ground. He had whittled that stick away to nothing. Probably he was very bored.

I wished I had a stick to whittle. I was bored too, but Kaye was almost bouncing with excitement. He kept looking at me and then looking back at the clearing and lifting his eyebrows. He was smiling so hard I thought his face was going to break. I leaned in for a closer look, hoping I could figure out what was going on.

The tall man shuffled over to the fire and stared at the short man for a few minutes. Then he frowned.

"Badger," he said, in an annoyed voice, "why don't you ever take off that stupid-looking hood and that smelly old scarf?"

I wondered how the short man had gotten the name Badger. Maybe it was because of his scruffy beard. Or maybe because of his smell. It was pretty strong. I've never picked up an actual badger and buried my nose in its fur and breathed in really deep, but I imagined it might smell like him. Badger's pungent odor blended with the smoke from the fire and the meaty smell of the stew and drifted up to us along with their conversation.

"I won't be taking off this hood or scarf for anyone, Rex, you stupid beanpole! They is *my* properties and I will do as I wants with them," cried Badger.

"Beanpole? I'm no beanpole! I am a good-looking man. The ladies all admire my height and my fine wide shoulders," snorted Rex. He picked up a big stick and loomed over Badger.

Badger started laughing. "Ladies! I don't see no ladies here. They don't admire you enough to come find you in this here miserable dripping forest so's they can stand there wringing their fingers together and sighing about them fine wide shoulders of yours. *Maybe* they isn't so wide as you think!" he cried.

"They most certainly is—I mean, are!" Rex said.

"Nay, nay," muttered Badger as he shook his head sadly. "Truth is, Beanpole, you're so skinny you could be squeezing right through the keyhole of the little queen's treasure house, but you wouldn't never be able to get back out again with them giant bags of gold because they'd get stuck in the keyhole and you'd be too stupid to let go of them!"

Rex turned dark red and then purple. He was shuddering with rage as he glared at Badger. Then he swallowed hard. Really hard, like there was a giant rock in his throat. Then he took a big swallow out of a flask—to help wash down the rock, I guess. His face went from purple back to dark red and back to its regular red.

"Enough about me," said Rex through clenched teeth. "Now are you going to take off that stupid hood and scarf or am I going to have to take them off for you?"

"I'd like to see you try, you big lout!" screamed Badger, bristling and snarling with fury.

He crouched down in the dirt like he was about to spring at Rex. He really did look like an angry badger. The rest of the gang of bandits was now awake and they gathered around to watch the fight.

Rex reached down and tried to pull off Badger's hood. Immediately Badger stomped down on Rex's right foot with one of his heavy nailed boots. Poor Rex wore light shoes that were good for sneaking through the forest. Rex yelped and started hopping around the clearing on his good foot while the other bandits laughed at him.

As soon as Badger had the chance, he snatched the flute out of Rex's belt. He poked Rex in the stomach with it as he was hopping around and Rex almost fell over.

Badger started blowing into the flute and making terrible noises while he annoyed Rex by asking, "Is this the song that you play for them beautiful ladies?"

In between notes, Badger jabbed Rex in the stomach with the flute, but he finally poked him too hard, and Rex was so clumsy that he lost his balance, fell backwards, and sat down in the pot of hot stew.

"Aaaugh! It's hot, it's hot, it's hot!" cried Rex, as the pain forced him to jump right back up again.

Badger rushed over to Rex and stomped on his other foot, and Rex gave another loud yelp and fell over backwards again into the puddle of stew.

Angry that Rex was wearing their only meal for the day, the rest of the men joined in the fight. They pummeled each other and tripped over one another, while Badger stood on the side, jumping up and down and shrieking awful things like, "Grab his beard, Tubby!" and "Poke him in the eyes, Rex!"

They were so clumsy and so bad at fighting that Kaye and I were laughing hysterically up in our leafy hiding place.

Suddenly the red-headed man, who seemed to be their leader, yelled out, "Stop fighting and shut up!"

Kaye and I stopped laughing.

"What is it, Crimson?" asked one of the men.

"Did you hear that?" said Crimson, "It sounds like someone's out there!"

It was suddenly deathly quiet. All of the men froze and looked our way. Rex's hand went to the knife in his belt. My heart started racing and I grabbed onto the branch below me with both hands. What if they found us?

Just then Kaye poked me really hard and pointed at Rex. I couldn't figure out why he was doing this again right now, so I scrunched up my face and shrugged at Kaye. He pointed to his own neck and then pointed at Rex again.

Finally I realized what Kaye had been so excited about all this time. I saw the compass pouch hanging around Rex's neck. He was so close I could see the square outline of the compass inside of it. At last I knew where it was!

Crimson and Badger crept to the edge of the clearing. They were almost underneath us. Crimson gripped a thick wooden stick with strong fingers and Badger looked ready to pounce. He stepped on a twig and it cracked and my heart jumped up so high in my chest that I almost choked.

No one breathed.

Then Badger broke the silence, saying, "Aw, there's nothing out there, you dimwits!"

"Who's calling who dimwit?" yelled Crimson. And suddenly everyone was fighting again, louder than before. I guess no one liked being called a dimwit.

Kaye and I slid down the tree and slipped away when the noise was loudest. They never saw us leave.

As soon as we were out of earshot, we took off running. I remember watching Kaye run ahead of me. The net kept falling off his shoulder as he ran and he had to keep pushing it back up. Finally we were far enough away that we were safe.

"Kaye, he has the compass!" I cried, completely out of breath.

"I know! I saw it! I *told* you we'd find it in the forest!" he said.

Then I had a sudden terrible thought. "Kaye, how are we ever going to get it back?"

chapter tweLve

Kaye put his hand on his chin and thought for a moment, but then his hand fell to his side and he shrugged.

"I don't know, Reggie. We don't know enough about them to make a plan. We'll just have to start watching them until we know their habits. Then we can make a plan," he said.

"Should we go back and watch them now?" I asked.

He shook his head slowly, "No, let's start tomorrow. We'll spend the whole day with those bunglers."

I laughed. "They sure are bunglers. They're so clumsy and bad at everything. I think we can get the compass back from them if we try."

Kaye nodded and said, "You know, since we don't have to watch the bunglers today, we could do something else instead…" He twisted his fingers in the net and looked at me hopefully.

We spent the afternoon in the fields near Kaye's village, trying to catch rabbits. Each time we almost had one, it got away, and Kaye was more determined than ever to catch one. I knew we would be trying again soon.

Sure enough, Kaye wore the net looped around his waist and shoulder again the next day, even though we were only planning to watch the bungling bandits.

They stayed in their clearing all day, and at one point, while they were all sleeping, I leaned over and whispered to Kaye, "Do you think we could take it while he's asleep?"

He shook his head. "If he woke up, he'd only have to yell, and all the others would wake up and get us. They might be bunglers, but they could still hurt us."

After dinner, they began an argument. They were out of food and drink and they needed to either buy or steal some more. Eventually they decided to stake out Perilous Trail the next afternoon and hope for a victim to come along.

When we heard this, Kaye and I rolled our eyes at each other. Nobody used Perilous Trail. These bunglers weren't going to find anything to steal on that road.

However, at least we knew where they would be, and so the next afternoon, we were gliding through the shadows next to the road, searching for the bungling bandits.

Suddenly, we heard the sound of a galloping horse. A moment later, it came into view and we caught sight of the rider. It was a boy, a little older than Kaye and me, riding a beautiful animal and wearing expensive clothing. His hair was dark and his smile was big and he looked like a young king. It was dim in the woods, but he seemed to ride in his own patch of sunlight as he raced along.

Moments after he passed us, the bunglers sprang out of the wood, ambushed the young man, and had him dead to rights!

"Kaye," I said, "we have to do something!"

"Do you have any ideas?" Kaye said, although I could tell by the hand on his chin that he was already working on it.

"No," I was forced to admit.

At that moment, Kaye raised his eyebrows with his eyes wide open and said, "I've got it! We'll use the fishing net. Follow me."

We crept down the side of the road toward the bunglers and stopped behind a large oak whose big limbs stretched out over the robbers in the road below. Crimson had pulled the boy off his horse and thrown him to the ground. He lay in the dust and weeds of the road. Two of the gang were holding him down. The rest quickly pulled off the boy's rings, his fancy black coat, and his nice boots.

Rex was still holding up one of the boy's legs to admire his striped socks. I could hear him muttering, "I think I fancy these for meself. I think the ladies would fancy them on me too."

Badger snorted when he heard that, and in the meantime, the boy was shouting things like, "How dare you touch me!" and "I'll have the law on you!" until Badger gagged him. The boy still kept hollering through the gag, but I couldn't tell what he was saying anymore.

"Whatever we're going to do, we have to do it quickly," I said to Kaye. "They've just about finished robbing that poor boy."

"We have to climb the tree," Kaye said as he started clambering up the oak tree toward the big branch that stretched out over the road. I followed behind him. Then we inched our way along the branch until we were right above the highwaymen.

We looked down to see what was happening. Everyone was grouped together directly underneath us. The boy was still making yelling noises through his gag.

Badger leaned over the boy, "Enough of that noise now," he said, leering into the boy's face. "If you keep that up, there might be a nice shiny knight who comes along to rescue you, and then where would we be?"

Everybody laughed at that because of course there were no nice shiny knights anymore, except for Sir Henry, and he was in Eldridge.

Badger liked being the center of attention. He kept talking. "I'll tell you where we'd be. We'd still be waiting alone and sad with empty bellies to keep us company. But I tells you now, I hates the noise of an empty belly more than I hates the sound of your caterwauling!"

Rex and the rest of the gang were laughing at this when Crimson noticed that the boy's horse had disappeared somewhere down the road.

He was furious. "Idiots! We could have made good money selling that horse. It's worth a hundred times more than anything the boy's wearing. You fools let it get away!"

Kaye passed part of the fishnet to me.

Crimson frowned and glared at the boy. "Perhaps we'll have to see if anyone even wants this boy back. Someone cared enough to pay to dress him up like a popinjay. Maybe they would care enough to pay to get him back."

This was getting dangerous. Now they wanted to hold him for ransom. It was time to act. I looked at Kaye to see what he was planning.

"Reggie, I just thought of something," Kaye said.

"What?" I asked.

"This is the first time I've ever been up a tree and out on a limb by choice," he whispered back with his triangular grin showing.

"Argh! You always make the worst jokes at the worst times!" I said.

"Reggie," Kaye said, "don't you know humor helps ease a tense moment? Anyway, when I give the word, I want you to throw the net as hard as you can to the left."

"What word would that be?" I said, pleased with myself for coming up with a witty comeback.

"Any word!" Kaye said, with an annoyed expression on his face. I guess he was the only one allowed to make bad jokes. "Now pay attention!"

A moment later, Kaye yelled, "Now, Reggie, throw!" From up in the tree, it looked like a perfect throw, but the net only tangled up five of the six robbers.

Rex was still outside the net, and he pulled out his sword and glared up at us in the tree. Startled, I lost my balance and fell, only managing to catch myself at the last second so that I was dangling by one arm from the tree limb. The

boy couldn't help us, and the five other robbers were about
to free themselves from the net.

Kaye had to act fast. "Hold on, Reggie, I'll get you," he
said as he grabbed my arm and pulled it up so I could grab
the tree limb with both hands. Then without giving it a
second thought, Kaye jumped to the ground and stood toe
to toe with Rex.

It's true that Kaye knew how to use a sword, but unfortunately he didn't have one, so he pulled out his knitting needles and took a defensive position with a needle in each hand. "Defend yourself, you scallywag!" Kaye said, in a loud, confident voice.

At first, Rex was confused, but as soon as he realized what was going on he began to laugh uncontrollably.

CHAPTER THIRTEEN

"Are those knitting needles, boy?" Rex gasped between laughing breaths. Even the robbers in the net were laughing, but that was good because when they were laughing, they weren't trying to get out of the net.

"Would it make any difference if I said no?" Kaye asked.

Rex was laughing so loudly that he couldn't catch his breath and had to sit down in the road.

Without hesitating, Kaye whipped out his yarn and quickly wrapped it around Rex's hands and feet before he even knew what had happened.

By that time I was down from the tree and Kaye said, "Help me stop the others before they escape from the net."

"What do you want me to do?" I asked.

"Here," Kaye said, "take this, pull it tight, and tie it around the tree."

He handed me a loose rope at the edge of the net that acted like a drawstring, tightening around the bottom so the bunglers were stuck close together inside the net. Once I wrapped it around the tree, they couldn't really move, even though their feet and their bony ankles were sticking out of the bottom of the net. Kaye took out his knitting needles and started working at breakneck speed. Clickety-click, clickety-clack, one after another, Kaye knitted their ankles together in no time at all.

The boy stared at us with eyes as wide as the sky. I looked around at the struggling, shouting robbers in the net and Rex sulking in the road, and I knew exactly what to do next. I marched over to Rex, lifted the compass pouch over his head, and put it around my neck where it belonged. The leather strap had been broken and was tied back together, so it had probably fallen off my neck somewhere in the forest. Rex must have found it and repaired it. I was so relieved to have it back! Then I remembered why we had attacked the bunglers in the first place. I looked over at the boy.

"Well," I said, "I guess we should probably untie him."

We walked over to the young man, cut the bonds on his hands, and then loosened his gag.

The first words out of his mouth were, "Astounding! That was the most amazing thing I've ever seen! Where in the world did you learn to knit like that? Have you visited the southern countries? They have some very fine knitters there—or so I've been told." He spoke with an accent, which meant he was not born in Knox, which would explain why he was so foolish as to travel on Perilous Trail.

Kaye, rolled his eyes, but said nicely enough, "Before we talk about knitting, I think we should get out of here. These gentlemen are going to break free at any moment. Let's go."

I collected our new friend's expensive black coat and his fine leather boots and one of his socks. He was still wearing the other one. I handed the things to him and he looked at them for a moment. Then he pulled off his one remaining sock and draped both of them over Rex's face, so they hung down over his nose. Rex scrunched up his face.

The boy said to Rex, "Sir, since you liked the looks of my socks so much, I thought you might enjoy their delightful smell as well." He made a polite bow to Rex and then walked down the road in his bare feet, carrying his clothes.

Kaye and I raced to catch up with him. We walked in silence until we were out of sight of the robbers, and then Kaye insisted that we leave the trail and lose ourselves in the wood, in case the bunglers freed themselves and felt like chasing after us.

We headed for the tower trees. These were unusually tall trees that grew straight up for many feet before branching out. No one could climb them, but there was one ordinary tree growing next to them where it was possible to climb up very high and then get across to the tower trees.

Soon all of us were sitting comfortably in a row on a large branch in one of the tallest tower trees. The first thing I did was to check the compass. Thankfully, it still worked. After putting it away, I took bread and cheese out of my dinner bag and shared them with Kaye and the boy.

I had to ask him, "Why were you traveling on Perilous Trail? Don't you know that's a terrible idea?"

The boy grinned and replied, "Well, I know it now. But I'm safe, thanks to you two. I can't believe you defeated six of them armed only with knitting needles—how embarrassing for them."

He shook his head in disbelief. "I've never seen anything like that! You showed uncommon bravery in what you did, and extraordinary ability at knitting! Where did you learn how to do that? Knitting is such a rare craft, and produces the finest clothing fit for kings, and yet you use it to bind common criminals! I shall surely tell my aunt of your bravery and audacity."

Kaye finally took a bite of his bread and cheese. After he swallowed, he said, "My name is Kaye Balfour, and this is Reginald Stork. What's your name?"

"My friends call me Beau," he began, but before he could complete his introduction, he said, "Balfour, that name sounds familiar. Are you related to Sir Henry Balfour?"

"He's my father," Kaye said. "Why do you ask?"

"My aunt knows him. She speaks very highly of him. She says he's one of only a few good knights left in Knox," Beau said.

Kaye and I spoke at the same time, "Your aunt?"

Then Beau said, "Yes, my aunt, Queen Vianne."

For a wonder, Kaye was silent, but I couldn't let the mystery rest. "Wait, so that would make you..." I trailed off.

"Duke Beauregard, the queen's nephew."

Now I was struck silent. But Kaye immediately said, "Our most sincere apologies, Your Grace, we didn't know who you were."

"No need for apologies. You can call me Beau. After all you did save my life. Now tell me how you learned to knit," he said to Kaye.

Kaye explained to Beau about his grandfather and the knitting and why he wanted it to stay a secret, but Beau never actually promised that he would keep that secret.

We climbed down from the trees and soon found Beau's horse grazing in a field outside the forest like a sensible animal. When we parted ways a little later, all of us returned separately to our homes. We did not know it at the time, but soon the story of Kaye's adventures would reach the queen's ears, and when it did, nothing would ever be the same.

However, that was all in the future. That day, I simply ran back to Crofton with the compass around my neck, cradling it close to my chest with one hand all the way home.

chapter fourteen

Returning the compass was even easier than taking it had been. My father was occupied with his clerks because sheep-shearing time was the busiest time of the year for him. Everyone had wool to sell.

I strolled into the countinghouse, checked to make sure no one was nearby, and carefully placed the compass back into the box. Then I went home.

No one saw me, no one spoke to me, and no one even knew the compass had been gone. I should have been so happy, but part of me felt empty. Kaye would probably say it was because I felt guilty for doing something wrong and getting away with it, but I wasn't sure about that. All I knew for sure was that I was going to think twice before ever taking something else that didn't belong to me. I thought maybe I felt empty because I needed to eat, so I headed for the kitchen.

Everything was in an uproar there. A messenger had arrived from Lady Martha! He sat in a chair, looking battered and bruised. My mother fussed over him, preparing ointments for his scrapes and binding up his bruises with rosemary oil. The sharp, spicy smell filled the kitchen.

"What happened?" I cried.

The messenger grinned sheepishly. "I came from Goddard, with a message from Lady Martha. My group of travelers was attacked by bandits near the end of our journey, but I had nothing worth stealing, so they mostly left me alone."

"What did they look like?" I was afraid they might have been the bunglers.

He shrugged. "They were big men. There were maybe about twelve of them. I don't remember much more."

"Oh," I said. They couldn't have been the bunglers. "What was the message?" I asked.

"Are you young Reggie, then?" asked the messenger.

I nodded.

"It's about you. Lady Martha wants you to visit for the summer," he said.

"The whole summer!" I cried. "Mum! Do you think Father will let me go?"

She tied a bandage around the man's arm and said, "There, Thomas, I think that will help." Then she looked at me and said, "I don't know, Reggie. He might want you to stay home and work with your new tutor, but I suppose it's possible he'll let you go. He will be very honored that Sir Henry's wife wants you to visit."

Mum was right. Father was so impressed that I had a chance to get to know the family of the most famous knight in Knox that he agreed right away to let me go. He was excited because he hoped that knowing such important people would somehow help him continue to improve his business.

I was excited because I was going to spend the summer with my friend. For the first time in a long time, we were excited about the same thing, even if it was for different reasons.

Early the next morning, Thomas and I prepared to leave the city together. Mum hugged me good-bye about a hundred times and warned me not to trust strangers and not to eat too much and not to poke my nose in places where it didn't belong. Father told me to be polite and to make him proud.

For safety, Thomas and I were supposed to join a large group of travelers that was setting out on the two-day journey around the forest.

However, as soon as Thomas and I were alone, he turned to me and said, "Young Kaye hinted to me that I should ask you about a better way to travel to Goddard."

"What do you mean by a better way?" I asked.

"A faster way," he answered.

I thought about it for a moment, but then I decided if Kaye trusted Thomas, then I did too. "Follow me," I said. "This won't take long."

Thomas and I arrived in Goddard three hours later. I was looking forward to a long summer of riding, exploring, swimming in the river, and hiding from Charles Atwood, but instead, one of the most peculiar things to ever happen in the history of Knox happened to Kaye and me that summer. It all began a few days later, when a group of the queen's messengers rode into the courtyard of Sir Henry's castle.

chapter fifteen

The queen's messengers were a serious group of men in dark, plain armor, accompanied by a long-whiskered man wearing old leather.

One of the serious men spoke in a loud voice to the crowd of people that had gathered around. "We bring a message from the queen," he announced.

Lady Martha came forward, saying "I am Lady Martha. What is your message?"

He shook his head and said, "The message is for young Kaye Balfour."

In the midst of everyone's surprise, Kaye stepped forward and said, "I'm Kaye."

The man leaned down from his saddle and handed a letter to Kaye. It was sealed with the royal seal. Kaye opened it and read, "The queen requests the presence of Kaye Balfour and Reginald Stork at Castle Forte immediately."

Kaye and I knew right away that Beau had told the queen that we had rescued him from the bandits, but Lady Martha could not imagine why the queen would invite two boys she had never met to the castle.

"Kaye!" Lady Martha said, "This is very strange. Do you have any idea why the queen would invite you to court?"

"Well, Mum," Kaye said, "I, ah, might have an idea."

"Then speak up, boy. Why would the queen ask you to visit?" Lady Martha asked.

"Oh. Well, I think perhaps her nephew asked her to do that. We met him the other day," began Kaye.

"I did not hear that the young duke was visiting in these parts," Lady Martha said.

"Oh. No. No, he was, ah, not visiting. He was only passing by," Kaye said, looking uncomfortable.

Lady Martha narrowed her eyes.

"Kaye Aloysius Balfour! Tell me how and where you met the duke!"

So Kaye explained how we happened to have met Duke Beauregard traveling along Perilous Trail, and accidentally saved him from a few frail and clumsy highwaymen.

He tried hard to make it sound like it was nothing, but Lady Martha quickly figured out that Kaye had been spending every day doing exactly the thing he'd been told not to do—wandering through the Knotted Woods. Even when we explained that we had been working on making a map, it didn't help.

After she calmed down, Lady Martha decided that Kaye and I had to obey the queen and visit Castle Forte, but she couldn't decide whether to come with us or not. She was afraid to make the dangerous journey to Castle Forte, but at the same time, she was very curious to see what the new queen was like.

In the end, Lady Martha decided she would go with us. We left before sunrise the next day. The village was misty and still as we rode through it. The horses' hooves made sleepy thuds on the damp dirt of the road. We traveled close together in a quiet pack for protection against bandits.

The long-whiskered man was Alfred, the queen's own messenger. His face was brown and wrinkled like the bark of an oak tree, and his nose was big and knobby and very red, like he wiped it on his sleeve all day long, although we never caught him doing it. His long, fluffy, gray-brown beard grew down to his knees, and he combed it out every night with a wooden comb.

He was not an entertaining traveling companion. He never spoke. He only grunted. So there were no stories or songs to pass the time while he was around. Kaye and I started secretly calling him Old Stone Face.

Surprisingly, Old Stone Face knew every inch of the kingdom of Knox. He led us to Castle Forte by back ways and unknown trails that were so much safer than the regular roads that we arrived at the castle after only two days.

Kaye had visited the castle once before, when he was very young and the old king still lived. But I had never seen anything like this! There were two thick walls around this castle, each one with a gatehouse. After passing through these, Alfred led us into the main courtyard. The gardens and orchards and stables and dairies were much bigger than the ones at Kaye's father's castle. The queen's castle was huge and impressive, with tall round towers soaring up into the sky. The watchmen high up on the flat tops of the towers looked as small as birds.

Kaye's castle was a happy place with everyone busy at their work, but no one seemed happy or busy here. Even though the sun was shining, it felt gloomy. Hardly anyone was working, and the few people I saw hardly even picked up their feet as they walked. Some men dozed in the shade. The gardens were full of weeds. Even the animals looked tired and sad. I have never wanted to comfort a pig, but when I saw the pigs at the palace, I felt like they needed a friend.

Old Stone Face took us into the main entrance of the castle, and from there we entered the great hall. Dirt and dust and filth covered everything. The windows that weren't broken were too dirty to see through. The cavernous hall was filled with garbage—pieces of rusted armor, broken furniture, buckets, old cooking pots, spoiled food—the place looked like the treasure caves after a flood. I could hear rats and mice scurrying through the crumbling rushes on the floor. This was no place for a king or a queen. There should have been servants everywhere.

Alfred grunted at us and nodded toward the center of the room, and we sat down in the mess of furniture—Lady Martha on the only chair and Kaye and I on an upside-down chest. The silence in the room swallowed us up like a yawn, until we heard a soft tapping sound, like little footsteps coming closer and closer.

CHapteR SixteeN

A young lady appeared in the doorway. She carried a large metal bowl filled with water and some cloths on her arm, and she was beautiful. Her teeth were white and perfect, her hair was the color of honey, and her dress was blue like the sky. She even smelled good, like herbs from the garden.

She curtsied in front of Lady Martha and said, "Welcome, honored guests. You are Lady Martha, and this is Sir Henry's brave son and his brave friend, yes?" She spoke her words with the same foreign pronunciation that Beau used.

Lady Martha nodded.

The woman smiled and said, "Very good. I am Nicolette Longchamps, the queen's lady-in-waiting. We are most enchanted that you were able to come."

She held the bowl of water toward Kaye's mum, "Please, you have had a long journey. Wash your hands and I will take you somewhere more comfortable to wait. This room, it makes a bad taste in my mouth."

Lady Martha washed and asked, "What happened here?"

"Ah, the old king's servants, while he was ill, were not doing their duties to the good king," Nicolette said. "Many of them left. When we arrived, only two months ago, it looked like this. Alfred should never have left you to wait here."

When we had all washed, Nicolette smiled and said, "Please, leave the towels here and I will return for them later. It should not be me that does this, but there is no one else. Now, if you will follow me?"

Nicolette led us up some stairs and down a passage into a small room. "Please sit down and I will bring you something to eat. It is not yet time for dinner, but you have been traveling and will need a small meal," she said.

Someone had been scrubbing up here. The seats had soft cushions on them in bright colors. Some of the walls were freshly painted with flowers and others had tapestries hanging on them. Lady Martha sank into one of the seats with a sigh of pleasure.

Kaye and I rushed to the window to look out, but she called us back, "Boys! Sit down and wait. Remember to act like you are in a palace."

Nicolette returned, carrying a large dish that was heaped with little pies. Alfred plodded behind her, carrying a flagon of apple cider and some goblets. He set the goblets down on a table, filled each cup with exactly the same amount of liquid, and then trudged away.

Kaye and I came over to examine the pastries. Nicolette smiled and tugged lightly on my hair. "These, you will like. They are tourteletes—fried dough filled with spiced fig and brushed with honey."

She sat down by Lady Martha and said, "The queen is in council and will come when she can. It is hard for her. Eight of us came here together to Knox—my lady the queen, her nephew the duke, myself, four guardsmen, and a cook who is in love with my lady. His name is Abelard, and he cooks like no one else. We are most fortunate to have him with us."

"Did all the servants leave?" Lady Martha asked.

Nicolette nodded. "They fear the knights who stay here and do nothing but eat and drink and fight and sleep. They are all hungry, and they all dislike the queen very much, although they do not know her. It is fortunate Abelard cooks so well, or else they might make much trouble for the queen. Already Abelard has saved the life of his lady many times."

The fig pies melted in my mouth. Abelard must have loved the queen very much to make sweetmeats this delicious. Kaye and I had eaten half the plate of pies when we noticed that the ladies weren't paying attention to us any longer.

"Reggie," Kaye whispered, "Let's do some exploring."

I nodded with my mouth full and tucked a few pies into my shirt for later. Lady Martha did not notice us sneaking out of the room. She was very interested in Nicolette's story. "Surely the queen does not love him back?" she asked. "A queen could never marry a cook."

Nicolette laughed merrily. "Oh no. She loves his almond cream and his roasted beef, but she could never love him more than that. If she marries, she must marry a nobleman, of course. She is queen of this country and it is her duty."

We walked briskly past the ladies and left the room. Once we were in the hallway, we looked at each other and grinned.

CHAPTER SEVENTEEN

"Where should we explore first?" I asked.

"Everywhere!" Kaye said.

We wandered up and down stairways and through endless dusty passages and countless cobwebbed doorways. We found the library, where the king's precious books were broken and scattered across the floor. In the bedchambers, the bed linen was thrown about and the foul-smelling chamber pots had not been emptied for days.

In one place, we found a small couch under an open window. The dusty curtains and a ragged tapestry on the wall moved faintly in the cool breeze blowing through the window. It inspired me.

I looked behind the tapestry. "Kaye, I have another brilliant idea."

"What is it?" he asked.

"Let's hunt for a secret passage. We're sure to find one. There are always secret passages in castles," I said.

"Maybe we'll find one that even the queen doesn't know about, and someday we can tell her and surprise her," Kaye said.

We peered behind wardrobes and felt along the walls of the great, cold fireplaces filled with old ashes. We found nothing but dust and spiders. I was ready to give up when we discovered a large room with an entire wall of high pointed windows. It was decorated with enormous tapestries, odd statues, and a suit of old-fashioned armor.

"Kaye, this could be the place. Look at the tapestries. They're so big they must have something hidden behind them," I said.

I ran to the nearest tapestry and pulled on the bottom to see what was behind it. It was stuck, so I leaned back and put all my weight into it.

Suddenly I heard Kaye shout, "Reggie, let go. You're pulling too hard."

It was too late. The tapestry ripped and I went over backwards, striking my head hard against the wall as I fell. I felt a sharp pain in my head and I heard a thump and a breaking noise as I landed on the floor. When I opened my eyes, the room spun wildly around my head twice and then came to a slow stop.

After a few seconds, I sat up, rubbing the lump on my head, and I heard Kaye say in an unusually kind voice, "Poor lamb."

I stared at Kaye with my eyebrows scrunched together. "Are you talking to me?"

"No, why?"

"Because I'm hurt! I hit my head, in case you didn't notice! And it HURTS!" I yelled at him. It really did hurt, although it was already better than it had been a few seconds earlier.

"Reggie, you're fine. You can sit up and you can yell and you'll be fine. But look at this," he said.

I looked and discovered that when I fell, I had knocked down a wooden stand with a stone statue on top of it. The statue had broken into two pieces, right across the middle.

It was a statue of a lamb standing up on its hind legs. It looked like an ugly, fat, wooly little boy with a sheep's face. I should have known Kaye was making the wrong joke at the wrong time with his "poor lamb" comment.

"What are we going to do?" I whispered. "What if that was the queen's special ugly sheep statue?"

"Let me think," he said. He put his hand on his chin and a moment later, he said, "I've got it. Help me lift this, Reggie."

We put the tall wooden pedestal back where it belonged, and set up the statue on top of it. The lamb wasn't very big, so it was easy to hold on to it, but it was heavy and hard to lift over our heads. Once the top half was resting on the bottom half, it looked almost normal, except for the big crack across the middle.

"How can we keep it from falling off again?" I asked.

"Watch," Kaye said. He swiftly knit a kind of wide belt that he wrapped tightly around the crack. The gray of the yarn disappeared against the gray stone.

"There," Kaye said, "that ought to keep it in place."

"That's perfect," I said. "From far away, you can't even tell he's wearing a belt. But what about the tapestry?"

"That," Kaye said, "is even easier to fix. Look!" He knotted a strand of yarn to a few of the loose threads of the tapestry and began to knit. Every stitch or two, he tied some more of the loose threads to the yarn. In a few seconds, I couldn't even see the tear. The yarn didn't match, but it was close to the ground. Probably no one would ever see it.

"Good work, Kaye," I said, "but I still want to look behind the other tapestries before we go."

We easily pulled the next giant tapestry away from the wall and found a wide, arched space behind it. At the back of the space, there was a normal door—not a secret one—but it was half open and there were people talking on the other side of it. We crept into the dark space behind the tapestry for a closer look.

CHApter eiGHteeN

The room was full of men. Big men, wide men, tall men, strong men, hairy men, every sort of man you could imagine. A few of them were all those things. Some of them were playing with dice. Others were picking their teeth. One of them was eating an entire ham, holding it by the bone in his giant fist. Two others were having a belching contest.

Underneath all their noise, I could hear a woman's faint voice. We moved closer to the door in order to see her. She was small and dark-haired and she looked too thin, standing at the front of the room, shouting to make herself heard. Beau leaned against a wall near her, scowling at the crowd in front of him

Kaye pulled on my sleeve. "Reggie," he hissed in my ear, "that's the queen."

"It can't be," I whispered back. "If she was the queen, they would listen to her."

"It is the queen. And they're not even trying to listen." Kaye was getting upset.

Suddenly Beau grabbed a long trumpet off the wall and blew an angry blast on it. "How dare you!" he shouted. "This is your queen! You owe her your loyalty and respect. Do not forget that she can take away your lands."

After this threat, the men listened, but they still did not look interested in what the queen had to say.

"Knights of the kingdom of Knox," she said, while Kaye and I gaped at each other. We had never imagined that knights would act like this—not in front of their queen.

"This country needs its knights to protect and help the people. Show them fine examples of what real knights can be, and help me fix the troubles of Knox. You are the heroes of the people's stories, so I beg you to bring their heroes to life!"

I felt bad for her. None of these men would ever be a fine example of anything, except how to eat a ham as loudly as possible.

One of the dice-playing knights got to his feet and yelled across the room, "You want us to help you to fix the troubles of Knox? It's not even your country. You don't know anything about it."

"Yeah!" cried the others.

One of the belchers joined in, "How are you going to fix a country? You can't even run a castle! My chamber pot hasn't been emptied in days. There's no hall to eat in. You've failed at everything."

"YEAH!" the others cried.

"The food's good," said Ham-eater, but not many people could hear him, since his mouth was full.

The queen drew herself up as tall as she could and lifted one hand for silence. "I have not even begun to make changes in this castle or this country. All I ask is that you try to be the knights that the people want to believe you are. To help you do this, in one month I will hold a tournament and contests in the feats of arms, where you may show your knightly abilities to the people. The champions will receive much fame and glory and honor."

Someone called out, "We don't want to fight in a tournament. It's too much work!"

"Enough!" she cried, with her cheeks turning red. "You must participate in the tournament. If you do not, I will take your lands and give them to someone who *wants* to help the people of Knox. I am tired of your selfishness. I am determined to find some real knights, knights in whose valor I can rejoice. I see that I shall have to find them myself, because they are not here. I am ashamed of the knights of Knox."

She hurried from the room while Kaye and I stared at each other in amazement. Things were worse than we had imagined if the knights could treat the queen like this.

"I wish my father was here," Kaye said. "He would know how to fix this."

I nodded, but then said, "Kaye, I think the queen's on her way to meet us now. We had better get back."

"Well, let's go," Kaye said.

We raced back to the room where we had left Kaye's mum and although we were out of breath, she and Nicolette were deep in conversation and didn't notice that we had arrived—or that we had ever left, for that matter.

chapter nineteen

Moments after we returned, Beau walked into the room. He looked tired, but his face lit up with his giant smile when he saw us.

"Kaye, Reggie, I'm glad you're here," Beau said. "I told the queen how you saved my life, and about your astounding skill with knitting. She just had to meet you and see your knitting for herself."

Lady Martha looked down at Kaye as if to say with her eyes, "What else did you forget to tell me?" He looked away, a little guiltily.

Beau bowed to Kaye's mum. "Lady Martha, it's an honor to meet you. If you will come with me, I'll take you to the queen's private rooms, where she will be enchanted to meet you."

He led us into a large, airy room that was rich with carvings, tapestries, and stained glass windows. A few minutes later the queen entered the chamber along with four palace guards. She sat on the throne and two guards positioned themselves on either side of her. Nicolette stood behind her.

The rest of us knelt before her and murmured, "Your Majesty." Now that I could see her more closely, I could see that her hair was a dark brown color, and her eyes were the

same color as Nicolette's dress. But her face was pale and there were heavy shadows under her eyes.

The queen said to Kaye's mum, "Lady Martha, thank you for coming to see me. I have wanted to meet you because your husband is a good, trustworthy man. I wish that I did not need him to stay in Eldridge, but that he could come home and be with his family. I'm sure you feel the same. I thank you for your patience while he is gone."

Lady Martha was surprised and pleased by the queen's thoughtfulness. "He must do his duty as a knight of Knox, Your Majesty. I understand. But I do miss him," she said.

The queen nodded. "We shall do our best to bring him home as quickly as possible. It has been a long time already, has it not?"

"Two years, Your Majesty," Lady Martha whispered.

The queen sighed. "I'm sorry for that," she replied. "But you may take comfort in knowing that he has done great good in keeping the peace between Knox and Eldridge."

Next she looked at Kaye. "You must be young Kaye Balfour," said the queen, turning to me, "and you must be Reginald Stork."

I was overwhelmed. Queen Vianne wasn't as pretty as Nicolette and she was much quieter, but if you saw them next to each other, you would know right away which one was the queen.

"Um, yes, Your Majesty. And, um, no, Your Majesty. I— I'm just Reggie," I stammered. I couldn't stop looking at her. I understood why Abelard the cook came all the way from Vinland just to be near her.

I must have sounded foolish, because Kaye said. "Yes, Your Majesty. I'm Kaye and this is my friend Reggie. It is an honor to be here."

"My nephew cannot stop talking about how you saved his life from the highwaymen, and I wished to thank you personally," said the queen.

Suddenly her stiff ways disappeared as she smiled a warm, friendly smile at Kaye. "And I do thank you. I'm so grateful that you were able to save Beau. It would have been a terrible beginning to my life here in Knox if I had lost him. Thank you for your kindness, Kaye Balfour, and for your chivalry. It is a rare gift."

I could tell that because of Queen Vianne's kindness, Kaye, like Abelard and me, was ready to follow her anywhere. I think he would have done anything for her, and what happened next proved it to me.

She continued talking, "Beau also told me that you have an extraordinary skill with knitting, and as unusual as that sounded, I wanted to see it for myself. So please, young Balfour, show me your talents."

Kaye nodded and pulled out his needles and yarn and started knitting away. Clickety-click, clickety-clack, faster and faster after every loop, he made a narrow bracelet and knelt as he offered it to the queen.

"I thought my nephew exaggerated your skill with the needles, but this is even more amazing than what he described!" said the queen. "Tell me, young Balfour, what do you plan to do with this gift of yours? I am most curious. You could be a wealthy man with a talent like yours."

Kaye frowned. I could tell that he wanted to please the queen, but that he also had to tell her the truth. "Your Majesty, I will knit only when it is needed, because what I want most is to be a knight like my father." He blushed after his bold words and looked down at the floor.

She smiled. "It is a worthy goal. To be sure, you have a gift of knitting, but as you showed when you rescued Beau, you also have the gift of chivalry, as all true knights do. I am sure you have much to learn about being a knight, but it may be that you also have much you can teach."

The queen paused and looked thoughtful for a moment, staring hard at Kaye. It became a long moment of silence. Then it became a very long moment of silence. I was sure I was going to sneeze.

Suddenly she stood up and called to Beau, "Bring me my sword," she commanded.

chapter twenty

Beau opened a chest and brought the queen a large sword with curling designs of gold and silver vines on the handle.

My mouth must have fallen open in surprise that this small queen had her own sword, because she glanced at me and said, "This sword was my father's. If he had not died when I was still a child, he would be ruler here today instead of me."

I couldn't think of anything to say to that. I shut my mouth instead.

Queen Vianne moved in front of the throne and gestured for Kaye to come to her. "I have made the decision to knight you, Kaye Balfour. Your services to the crown will be voluntary until you are older, but I believe you will do the kingdom of Knox much good, just as your father does. Lady Martha, are you agreeable to this?"

Lady Martha was startled by the suddenness of the queen's question. She hesitated. "He will not be in danger?" she finally asked.

"I will do my best to keep him safe," said the queen. "I will not allow him to fight with grown men, even in fun."

It took Lady Martha a long time to answer the queen. Kaye stared at her, begging with his eyes for her to say yes.

Finally Lady Martha said, "Yes. His father wishes him to be a knight, and while his father is away, Kaye cannot receive the training he needs. Perhaps he may receive such training here."

The queen turned to Kaye, "And you, Kaye Balfour, are you agreeable to becoming a knight of the kingdom of Knox?"

He fell on his knees before her and lifted up his face to say, "Yes, Your Majesty."

Queen Vianne touched Kaye lightly on his shoulder with the flat of the blade, and said, "I dub thee Sir Kaye Balfour, youngest knight of the land of Knox. Rise, Sir Kaye. Use your many gifts in behalf of the people of Knox, and you cannot fail."

It was so quiet that I could have heard a spider's footsteps. Lady Martha sniffed.

Unfortunately, the palace guards started to snicker, muttering to each other. "He is no knight. This scrawny brat could never face a real knight."

"Be silent!" snapped the queen with flashing eyes.

Kaye turned bright red and said to the queen, "Your Majesty, all the boys of my village used to laugh at the idea of me becoming a knight. And now, although I am honored to be knighted by you, I am afraid people will now laugh at me for *being* a knight, unless I prove my worthiness."

"I assure you, young Balfour, that you have already proven your worthiness to me by saving my nephew," said the queen.

"Thank you, Your Majesty!" Kaye said. "But I must prove my worthiness to the people as well."

"How will you do that?" the queen asked.

"I would like to compete in a tournament and the contests of the feats of arms," Kaye said.

"I plan to hold a tournament in a month's time, but you are very young to enter such contests," said the queen. "You would be competing against strong and experienced knights. Are you certain this is what you want to do?"

"Yes, Your Majesty, I'm certain," Kaye said.

"You will need a mentor to give you guidance," the queen said.

Duke Beauregard spoke up. "I will be Kaye's mentor, Your Majesty."

Looking intently at Kaye and his determined expression, the queen then said, "You have my blessing, Sir Kaye, with Beauregard as your mentor. But understand this, Kaye Balfour: you will not be permitted to compete in jousting or sword fighting or anything else that brings you into direct contact with any of the other knights. They are full-grown men, and they could easily crush you into a jelly."

"I understand, Your Majesty, thank you!" Kaye said.

The queen dismissed us, and we left the room, our heads spinning with surprise, as if we had all fallen backwards while pulling on a tapestry and struck our heads against a wall.

chapter twenty-one

Lady Martha returned home, but Kaye and I stayed at the castle so he could prepare for the tournament and contests. Beau was overjoyed that we were going to be his guests. That first morning he said to us, "Reggie, Kaye, I'm happy you are going to stay for a while. This castle needs people. Nicolette said to take you to your room first, so follow me," he said.

Our room was halfway up one of the tall towers. I was excited about sleeping so high off the ground until I realized this room was a dusty mess like the rest of the castle. Beau's face fell, but only for a moment. His big smile soon flashed into view again.

"I'm sorry about this room. We will have to fix it, but I've had lots of practice. As soon as we arrived in Knox, we had to fix up the queen's rooms and a few others. They all looked like this," he said.

There was nothing in the room but a large wooden bed with no bottom and no cushion to sleep on, an empty wardrobe, and two broken chairs.

Nicolette hurried into the room with brooms and brushes and buckets. She looked around and sighed.

"Well, my friends, I think we must start, or we will never finish this. Beau, you are tallest, you will clean the walls. Sir

Kaye, you will clean the floors. You will be this country's first scrubbing knight. And Reggie, as you are much the smallest, you will clean the bed and wardrobe," she said, smiling.

I didn't smile. I was only a tiny bit smaller than Kaye.

We scrubbed and polished all day. We even whitewashed the walls. While the four of us struggled to stretch a net of ropes tightly across the bottom of the bed to hold a mattress, the queen herself came in and painted some trees and vines with flowers on the bright white walls. Then Nicolette disappeared and came back with some of the kitchen boys. They carried a mattress, and she brought linen for the bed.

"Here, boys, put the mattress in the bed. Your Majesty, I am afraid there were no feathers with which to stuff it, but the cook, he said to use clean straw, and the kitchen boys, they helped me fill it. I hope it will be enough," Nicolette said.

The queen smiled and said, "I'm sure it will be enough, thank you, Nicolette."

The boys settled the mattress on the net of ropes and went back to the kitchen.

"Now it's time to test it!" I cried, and Kaye and Beau and I jumped into the big bed all at one time. The ropes under the mattress creaked, but they stayed strong.

"Ah!" Nicolette cried, laughing. "Nothing breaks! We have done well."

"But is it comfortable?" the queen asked. Beau snored loudly to answer her question, but I thought he only got away with that because he was her nephew.

"Yes, it's very nice," Kaye said to the queen. But since he was lying across the bed on his back and she was standing next to it, he was looking at her upside down. A moment later, he tumbled off the bed and stood next to her and bowed.

"I mean, yes, thank you, Your Majesty," he said.

Queen Vianne sat on the edge of the bed, pushing Beau's leg out of the way. She patted a spot next to her for Kaye to sit down.

After he sat, she said to him gently, "Sir Kaye, I am grateful for the respect you show to me. I know it is real, not just something you do to impress me. But Nicolette, she is like my sister, and Beau, the young rascal, is already my nephew. I hope that perhaps when it is only the five of us together, we may be more like a family and less like a royal court."

Kaye nodded. "Yes, Your Majesty. But when there are others nearby, I will still show you all the respect that you deserve—even if no one else does."

"I know you will, my friend. I just hope it does not prove to be a danger for you," replied the queen.

CHapteR tweNty-two

Beau and Kaye started training early the next day in the courtyard by the stables. Kaye had already learned many things from his father, but what he needed most was practice.

"I think we should start with sword fighting," Beau said.

"Why?" I asked. "The queen won't let Kaye do any sword fighting in the tournament."

"I know," Beau said, "but it's still good for him to practice as much as he can. A knight must know how to fight."

Kaye frowned and said, "My father says that fighting must always be the last thing a knight does. He says that a good knight must always try to use his head before using his sword..."

Beau interrupted him by saying, "Yes, but if that doesn't work, you still have to know how to fight! And if everyone already knows you are skilled with a sword, they are much more likely to listen to your words!"

"He's right, Kaye," I said. "Your father does all those things you said, but everyone knows he's good with a sword."

Kaye looked thoughtful. "I guess you're right," he finally agreed.

"Good!" cried Beau. "I have some practice swords in the stable."

They began to practice. I let Kadar out of the stable so he could watch them, and I think he enjoyed it. He paid close attention to their every move. I laid across an old haystack on my stomach and watched too. They weren't doing too badly. I pulled a piece of bread and some cold pork from where I had hidden them in my shirt sleeve earlier, and began eating.

A few minutes later two knights entered the courtyard and strolled across it, peering at Kaye and Beau as they approached. One of them was thin and sneering. His face was pinched-looking, like he only ate vinegar and sour plums. The other man was twice his size and smiled too much.

Just then, Beau pulled off a good move and made Kaye drop his sword. It clattered loudly on the stones as it fell.

The sneering knight scoffed with exasperation and said to the other knight, "This is exactly what I expected. I don't know what she was thinking, knighting this runt of a boy. She thinks she's teaching us a lesson, but she's only making a fool of herself, and this boy will ruin the entire kingdom. Mark my words, Melchor, you'll see it happen."

"Come now, Oliphus," said Sir Melchor. "Have you never dropped a sword?"

Melchor's voice was rich and smooth, like he soaked it in oil every night. He was tall and broad and had a big belly hanging over his belt. Unlike the other knights, he wore rough peasant clothes made of woven wool and had a short bristly black beard. Maybe Melchor didn't care about doing what everybody else did.

Kaye said, "I was just practicing, Sirs. I must practice if I am to get better." The tips of his ears were turning red.

Melchor was pleased by Kaye's answer. "That's right, my boy. There's nothing like practicing to make you better. Oliphus, this boy's a hard worker, you can see that for yourself. There's no harm in letting him play at being a knight."

Oliphus curled up his pinched lip. "He shouldn't be a knight. Other kingdoms will hear of this and think Knox is easy prey and they will invade and conquer. The queen's own people will think she is crazed and they will rebel, you'll see! Now that she's had that cursed proclamation read throughout the country, there's no way to hide what she's done."

"What proclamation is that, Sir?" Beau asked.

"The one announcing the tournament. It's been read in every city and village of the kingdom. It also proclaims the knighting of a puny, ferret-faced boy who thinks he can compete against real knights. She's a fool, and now everyone knows it. There is no hope left for Knox," Oliphus whined as he trailed off toward the castle.

Melchor laughed and said, "Don't mind him, boys. He is more upset about the proclamation than about young Kaye, here. It makes him turn sour."

While he spoke, he tenderly picked up my crumbs with his stubby fingers and scattered them on a low wall nearby where some little birds were making a fuss over each other.

"Here you are, my pretty birds," he said. They flew far away. Even Kadar kept one eye very carefully on Melchor at all times. He didn't move his head, but as Melchor walked around, sometimes I could see the whites of Kadar's eyes as he followed Melchor's movements.

"What else was in the proclamation, Sir Melchor?" I asked.

"Oh, mostly what Oliphus said. There will be a tournament, with jousting, but there will also be contests among the knights in the smaller knightly graces, like acrobatics and hawking and archery."

"Do we have to enter all the contests?" Kaye asked.

Melchor shook his head. "We only have to enter three contests, and one of them can be the new one that the queen named in her proclamation. That's the one that has Oliphus so nervous."

"What is it?" Kaye asked.

"No one knows," Melchor answered. "It is only named 'The Challenge of the Chivalrous Tales of Old,' and it says no more than that except that the winner will be declared Knox's favorite knight. Oliphus thinks that for this contest the queen will be asking questions to see which knight knows the most about the old stories. What do you think?"

Melchor asked Beau this last question, and as he did so, his eyes narrowed. He looked as clever as a bushy black fox, and I realized he was only being nice to us because he thought Beau knew some kind of secret about this mysterious contest. Melchor was a foul, sneaking cur who laughed too loudly so no one would notice what he was really like. No wonder the animals didn't like him.

Beau shook his head and said, "I have no idea. I never heard anything about it until you told me."

"Ah, well, we will all find out together, then," said Melchor. "But I think I will have a try at this contest. I should be Knox's favorite knight. After all, I am the best there is. Ask anyone. No one in the kingdom can beat me at jousting."

"I thought Sir Henry was Knox's favorite knight," I said to Melchor, which was a very bad idea.

He turned bright red and his eyes started to bulge. He picked me up by the shoulders and lifted me up so I was as tall as he was, with my legs dangling in the air beneath me. He squeezed my shoulders in his huge hands until I was afraid he was going to burst me like a blister.

"Sir Henry is not here," he hissed through his teeth. His breath was hot and he was so angry he was shaking. "And he is not going to be here for a very long time. I am just as good a knight as he is—in fact, I am better! You will see! Everyone will see! And I will win great fame and become Knox's favorite knight in this new contest!"

He dropped me to the ground in a little heap and stomped back to the castle.

chapter twenty-three

"Are you all right?" Beau asked me.

"Yes," I said as I moved my shoulders around. "I didn't fall very far, but he squeezed me really hard. He's strong."

"He's crazy," Kaye said.

Beau sat down near me and said, "What could it be? What are the 'Chivalrous Tales of Old?'"

"Oh, that's easy," I said. "Chivalrous tales of old Knox are always about Sir Gregory. He's the best knight that ever lived in Knox."

Kaye nodded. "It's true. I've heard all the stories. My grandfather likes to tell them on winter evenings in the hall to everyone who will listen."

"I've never heard of Sir Gregory," Beau said.

"You're not from Knox," I said.

"Tell me one," Beau begged. "Please!"

Kaye and I looked at each other. I guessed it was up to me. I decided to tell the story that everyone in Knox knew from the time they were babies.

"Well, long ago, in the golden days of old," I began, "Sir Gregory, The Lady's Knight, was called upon to rescue yet another fair maiden from the clutches of the terrible Lord Gromwelt."

"Yet another one?" Beau asked. "How many fair maidens did he have to rescue?"

"Hundreds," Kaye said. "And they all thought he would marry them after he rescued them. My grandfather says that after a while, Sir Gregory had to get married for his own protection, because once he actually had a wife, he didn't have to try to think of excuses not to marry the ladies he rescued."

"What happened to his wife?" Beau asked.

"Nothing. She stayed home while he kept rescuing other ladies from monsters and villains and dragons," Kaye said.

"Sounds boring. Were there really dragons in Knox in the old days?" Beau asked.

Kaye shrugged. "I don't know. It was the golden days of old. Maybe things were different back then, or maybe people had better imaginations."

"Will you *please* let me tell the story?" I yelled.

"Sorry," they both muttered.

I began again. "Sir Gregory went to rescue the fairest of maidens, the Lady Violetta, from the Brown Castle in the Knotted Wood."

"Why was it brown?" Beau asked.

"It was just built out of brown rocks. They came by boat from another country," Kaye said.

"Is it still there? The Brown Castle?" he asked again.

"I don't know. It's not in any of the places we've explored," I said. "But he was on his way to the Brown Castle when the villainous Lord Gromwelt released a thousand hungry wolves behind Sir Gregory. They were miles away, but he could hear them coming, and he ran faster and faster through the Knotted Wood, hoping to reach the Brown Castle before they were upon him."

"Where did this Gromwelt scoundrel keep a thousand wolves?" Beau asked.

"In a hidden cave in the mountains," Kaye answered.

"It must have been a big cave. Well then, what did he feed them?"

"AARGH! He *didn't* feed them. That's why they were so hungry. That's why they were chasing after Sir Gregory! They wanted to eat him." I said.

"That's a bit hard for the wolves, isn't it? I mean even if they ate Sir Gregory, he couldn't have fed more than a few of them. They'd still be hungry after catching him, don't you think?" Beau asked.

I sighed and said, "They were *bad* wolves. You don't have to care if they had enough to eat."

"I don't know, Reggie. He might be right," Kaye said. "Maybe that's why they were bad. Maybe if they had enough to eat, they would have been better wolves. I think there are good wolves. There are good people. Why not good wolves?"

I acted like they hadn't said anything and kept telling the story. "As he ran through the forest, next to the river, suddenly he couldn't move. Long snaking vines had twined themselves tightly around his ankle. But these were no ordinary vines. Even his famous sword Celestor could not cut through them. Sir Gregory was trapped!"

I was happy to see that everyone was finally being quiet and listening to my story, so I kept going. "Just then, an old woman of the wood passed by and said to him, 'Sir Gregory, at the bottom of the river there is a sword that can cut these vines, but you must find it yourself. Be warned, Sir Gregory. Only a true-hearted knight can find and use this sword.' Then she disappeared into the forest."

Beau started to open his mouth, but I glared at him until he was quiet again.

I continued, saying, "The vines were long enough that he could dive into the river, so he plunged into the freezing water and swam to the bottom. He couldn't see anything, but he used his hands to reach and reach and reach—until finally, he felt a sword! He swam up to the air and cut himself free just in time, because the wolves were almost upon him! He raced to the Brown Castle and rescued the Lady Violetta from the evil Lord Gromwelt and all was well again in Knox."

For a moment everyone was quiet, but then Beau said, "How did the sword know Sir Gregory was a true-hearted knight and that it should be found by him?"

I shook my head and said, "I don't know. Maybe the sword didn't know anything. Maybe he was able to find the sword because he *was* a true-hearted knight. Maybe true-hearted knights work harder than bad-hearted ones."

Beau nodded. "You know, there might be something to that idea."

Kaye started making jabs with his sword at the air, and then he looked back at us and said, "I wonder what happened to the wolves?"

chapter twenty-four

We decided that Kaye would enter the contests for horse riding, archery, and the mysterious Challenge of the Chivalrous Tales of Old. We hoped that the Challenge would be so new and surprising that no one would be very good at it.

All three of us practiced archery together. We shot at targets set up in a field. Beau was really good at it. He loved hunting, and to hear him talk, it sounded like hunting was the only thing he ever did back in Vinland. He could always hit the targets right in the middle.

I loved archery. I liked pulling back the string close to my ear and hearing it stretch tight until I could feel it had reached just far enough to make the arrow fly! I could usually hit the targets too. So could Kaye. Beau thought Kaye would do well enough in the archery contest.

Kaye also spent time each morning riding Kadar and practicing things like jumping and racing and making short turns. Kadar knew what he was doing and enjoyed showing off. Kaye's job was to stay on Kadar, although Kadar was obviously the one who was in charge. Even I could see that, and I wasn't very good with horses.

On the evening before the tournament, Beau called us into his room.

"Reggie, Kaye, come see what I have for you," he said.

I ran into his room with Kaye right behind me. "What is it?" I asked.

"I have gifts—one for Kaye and one for you," Beau said. He handed me a perfectly-shaped little short bow with a quiver of arrows. I pulled the string tight and when I let it go, it made a beautiful twanging noise.

"Thank you, Beau," I said. "It sounds just like music."

He laughed. "It can be your one-stringed lute, Reggie. Kaye, see what I found for you."

He opened a small wooden chest and lifted out the shining breastplate of a rather small suit of armor. "A knight needs a suit of armor. This used to be mine. There's a sword too. My uncle had it made for me when I was younger, but I think it can be made to fit you now. I also had a coat of arms designed for you and painted on your armor. I hope you like it."

"Thank you so much, Beau," Kaye said in a quiet voice.

He took the breastplate from Beau and looked closely at what was now his very own coat of arms—not his father's—not his grandfather's—but his very own. It was a simple blue color with a white eagle in the middle. Above and below the eagle were narrow white lines that I had to stare at very closely. I couldn't be sure, but it seemed like they were narrower at one end, so that they were almost pointed.

"Beau! Are those knitting needles?" I asked.

Beau grinned. "They certainly are," he said.

"Why knitting needles?" Kaye cried. "You know I don't like people to talk about me and knitting."

"No one will know, Kaye," I said. "You can't tell unless you look really closely."

"It's just for a joke, Kaye," Beau said. "I didn't think you'd mind. No one ever has to know but the three of us, I promise."

Kaye was smiling really big. "Well, I'm not going to tell anyone. And this is wonderful. Now everyone will see that I can be a real knight!" he said.

Beau shook his head. "Kaye, a real knight does his job and does what is right and doesn't worry about what other people think of him. He knows what he has to do and he does it."

Kaye looked at Beau. "That *sounds* good, Beau, but I don't know what to do, not really. Especially not in the Challenge of the Chivalrous Tales of Old. I don't know what it is, and I don't know what to do about it."

Beau took the armor and put it back in the chest, but as he did so, he looked up at Kaye and said, "You'll find a way to do what you have to do. I know it."

CHAPTER TWENTY-FIVE

The sun shone bright and clean on the first day of the tournament. Everyone was excited because this was the first tournament that had taken place in Knox in years.

It was held in a grassy field next to the castle. People were arriving early to get a good place so they could see. The ladies and the noblemen sat high above the ground in the stands, under a cloth canopy that protected them from the sun's heat. The queen's throne was set in a place of honor in the middle of the front row. Brightly colored flags and pennants dripped from the edges of the grandstand like melting wax drips down a candle. The villagers and servants sat below on wooden benches or stood in front of the stands.

Right in front of the audience was the lists, which was the name of the fenced-in place where the jousting and other contests would be held.

Behind the lists, the tournament helpers had set up colored striped pavilions, which were bright tents for the knights. Each knight had his own tent that he could go to between contests where he would rest or eat or put on his armor or even take off his armor—because for many of the contests, such as hawking and acrobatics, the knights didn't need to wear armor at all.

Kaye was not entering any contests where he needed to wear armor, and we spent the morning inside his little tent, waiting for something to happen.

"Why does it always take so long for things to start? Nothing is happening!" I complained.

Kaye shrugged. "Maybe it's hard to get all those people into their seats. They've been arriving since yesterday. All the inns in the city are filled. There will be a lot of people watching the tournament over the next few days," he said.

"Are any of your contests today?" I asked him.

"Only one, but it's later. So there isn't much to do right now. Maybe we could try putting on my armor a few times, just to get used to doing it," he said. "I wish I could wear it today. I'd feel more like a real knight." He sighed and looked at me. "I really wanted to wear it. Do you think I would look like a fool if I wore it even though I don't need it?"

"Yes, you would," I answered. "But we can try to figure out how to put it on anyway. There's nothing else to do."

I knelt on the ground and opened up the chest and just as I started pulling out the pieces, Beau entered the tent.

"Ah, Reggie," he said, "I don't think that armor will fit Kaye yet. We'll need to have an armorer or even a blacksmith do some work on it first."

Kaye's face drooped. I guess he really liked his armor. Beau noticed this too.

"But look what I have here," he said. "I was afraid it wasn't very nice to give you armor that you can't even wear yet, so I begged Nicolette to make this and she just finished it this morning."

He handed something made of cloth to Kaye, and Kaye held it up. It was a fine tunic, with Kaye's crest on the front in blue and white.

"It's just right, Beau, thank you! And tell Nicolette thank you," cried Kaye. He slipped it on over his other shirt and buckled his belt over it.

"It looks good," I said. "Not as good as armor, but it still looks good."

"I'll tell Nicolette. Maybe next time she can make you some armor, if that will make you happier," Beau said, as he tipped me over into the dirt and held me down.

Kaye was full of new energy now that he had his tunic with his own crest on it. He said excitedly, "Reggie, Beau, stop wrestling. Let's go see what's happening outside."

"We are *not* wrestling," I said with my face in the dirt. "I am being held prisoner. Set me free, you villain!" I yelled to Beau as I kicked at his boots. He let me go, and the three of us ran out into the fresh air and toward the crowded stands.

chapter twenty-six

We hadn't gone far when we met up with Sir Melchor. He was in a good mood. All the people passing by were telling their children how strong and powerful Sir Melchor was, and then the children stared at him with their mouths open. Melchor loved the attention.

"Well met, Sir Kaye, the smallest knight," he said cheerfully. "Are you looking forward to the contests today? Will I have the pleasure of jousting with you?"

His voice sounded pleasant, but his eyes were angry.

"N-no, Sir Melchor," Kaye said. "I am not jousting. I am only riding my horse in the horsemanship contest today."

"Ah, yes, your fine horse. He is a noble beast and worthy of carrying the finest warrior in the kingdom. Too bad he only has you," Melchor said in a nastier voice. I guess he was done pretending to be nice.

I had to say something. "He carries the son of Sir Henry, the finest warrior in the kingdom!" I cried. As usual, I should have kept quiet about Sir Henry in front of Melchor.

"He—is—not—HERE!" growled Melchor. "And after this tournament, everyone will see that I am the finest knight in Knox. I will win all the contests I enter, and that includes the Challenge of the Chivalrous Tales of Old!"

Kaye looked up at him, startled. I think he had been hoping that Melchor wouldn't be competing against him in that contest—or any contest for that matter.

Melchor nodded his head and smiled like a cat at dinnertime with a mouse under each paw. "Oh, yes, boy. We will be competing. In fact, we are the only two that will be entering that contest," he said. "And I will not be kind to you because you are young. I am here to win. If you get in my way I will squash you like a rotten fruit." He laughed again and strolled away.

Kaye looked at me and said, "Reggie, please stop mentioning my father to him. He hates my father, but I don't know why. My father is a good man."

"Sorry, Kaye," I mumbled. "I'll try not to do it again. But I get mad when he acts like your father is no good."

"He's just jealous," Beau said. "And he wants the prize from the Challenge of the Tales. The queen plans to give the winner a purse of gold and a medal and the title of 'The Knight's Knight.'"

"What is a knight's knight?" Kaye asked.

"Maybe it's the knight that rescues all the other knights!" I said. "Like the way Sir Gregory was called The Lady's Knight because he rescued all the ladies?"

Kaye frowned. "Knights don't need rescuing," he said.

"I know what it means," Beau said. "My aunt told me. She said that The Knight's Knight is the kind of knight that all the other knights should try to be like."

"Oh," I said. "That's not as interesting as rescuing people. And Kaye is good at rescuing people. Maybe you could ask the queen to change it?" I asked Beau.

He laughed and said, "I don't think so. The queen is very interested in having her knights follow a good example."

I thought about this for a moment. "Well, I hope you win anyway, Kaye. I think I'd like it better if the other knights tried to be like you instead of Melchor. He makes my teeth shiver. He's nice but he's mean at the same time. I don't understand him. And he smells worse than a dead rat."

Kaye looked at me thoughtfully and said, "Reggie, you are absolutely right. I hope that for the queen's sake, in some way and by some miracle, I can manage to win this contest."

"At least it's still a surprise contest for both of you," Beau said. "That way neither one of you will know what you're supposed to do ahead of time. Maybe that will help you win, Kaye."

Kaye looked worried. "I hope that's true," he said. Just then the trumpets blew, and the first day of the tournament officially began.

chapter twenty-seven

Watching the jousting that morning was loud and exciting and scary at the same time. The knights pointed their long lances at each other and then galloped toward each other as fast as possible. The idea was to knock the other knight backward off his horse. The one who stayed on his horse longest was the winner. Some of the knights were really good at staying on their horses, so sometimes the wooden lances splintered, and sometimes a piece of armor was knocked loose and went flying into the watching crowds. When that happened, people would rush to grab it, but I never knew if they kept it for themselves or if they gave it back later.

We had just watched Sir Dworfurd and Sir Fangle joust. Sir Fangle won, and afterward, a few of the tournament helpers had to carry poor Sir Dworfurd to the surgeon's tent. He was badly injured. Jousting was not a game. I was glad Kaye wasn't allowed to do it.

Melchor was one of the last knights to joust that morning. It was always easy to spot him. His shield was bright red with three blue boars and a gold lightning bolt on it. He won every joust.

On a little platform at the edge of the field stood the loudest man I had ever heard. He yelled out everything that happened during the contests so the crowd would know, and he declared that Sir Melchor would return to joust the next day.

That afternoon, Kaye competed in the horse riding competition. He and the other fifteen contestants each had their turn to show off their skills with horses. Beau and I watched from the side.

"He looks good enough, doesn't he, Beau?" I asked.

Beau nodded. "He's doing well. He's not the best rider, but he's not the worst rider either."

And Beau was right. Kaye didn't win first place, but he wasn't in last place either. Nobody paid much attention to him, and maybe that helped him to feel a little more comfortable when competing with all the grown men.

That night there was feasting and dancing in the city and all around the castle. Kaye and Beau and I joined in wherever we liked. Everyone was glad to have more guests. The only place that was dark and quiet was the castle itself.

chapter twenty-eight

The second day of the tournament was fine and bright like the first. It started with more jousting, and once again, Sir Melchor was one of the winners.

Kaye entered the archery contest that afternoon. As usual, Beau and I watched from the side as the tournament helpers set up targets and the archers entered the lists.

I pushed Beau with my elbow. "Beau, there are only three knights in this contest," I said as the two knights and Kaye took their places on a line. As they waited to begin, they adjusted their bowstrings and carefully looked at the target and felt to see which direction the wind was blowing.

He nodded his head and said, "I see that. Maybe it's good. Kaye will be sure to win at least third place."

"Oh, that's true," I said.

The other two knights were Sir Grumond and Sir Griswald. They shot their first arrows well, and so did Kaye. For the second arrow, the helpers moved the target farther away, and again all the knights shot their arrows into the center circles.

For the third and last arrow, the target was moved even farther away, and Sir Grumond and Sir Griswald shot first. Sir Griswald's arrow struck the very center of the target. Sir Grumond's arrow struck the edge of the center of the target.

Then Kaye lined up his arrow and drew back the string, and just as he let go, a breeze came out of nowhere and blew his arrow wide of the center, so it hit the outer edge of the target. The crowd roared, either with disappointment or laughter or because they were glad it was over. I don't really know why they made all that noise.

The loud man hollered out the names of the winners: "First place goes to Sir Griswald! Second place goes to Sir Grumond! Third place goes to the third archer, Sir Kaye, the youngest knight of the land of Knox to ever win a prize at a tournament!"

Now the crowd was laughing, although they were also crying "Hurrah!" I saw the queen smiling as the judge handed Kaye his prize, a small silver clasp for a cloak, and the helpers began clearing the lists for the next competition.

As we headed back to Kaye's tent, Sir Griswald came running up behind us and calling out, "Kaye! Sir Kaye!"

It was the first time any of the other knights had called him Sir Kaye without making a joke out of it.

Kaye turned to look at Sir Griswald. "Yes?" he said.

The knight was out of breath, and he panted, "I wanted to compliment you on your shooting—very well done—breezes happen to the best of us—I know your father—he would be proud." Sir Griswald clapped him on the back and wandered off.

"Well, look at that," Beau said. "There may be some good knights in Knox after all."

That night at our feasting and dancing, we were even happier than the night before. But the castle remained dark and quiet and still.

CHAPTER TWENTY-NINE

Finally the last day of the tournament arrived. All the crowd gathered to watch the Challenge of the Tales. Everyone wanted to find out what the mysterious contest would be.

The loud man explained how the contest would work. His name was Stentor and he bellowed loudly enough for Beau's mother to hear him back in Vinland.

"This contest is based on the tale of Sir Gregory's escape from the ravenous wolves of Sir Gromwelt and his rescue of a lady from the Brown Castle!" he said.

"Kaye!" I whispered. "That's my story! Why are the wolves ravenous in his story? They were only hungry in mine."

"It's the same thing," he whispered back. "Be quiet."

Stentor kept talking, "The lists have been prepared for the challenge."

He was right. The tournament helpers had dug a large ditch and filled it with water at one end of the lists. At the other end of the lists they had put up two strong tall poles. One pole was a little bit closer to the ditch than the other one. At the top of each pole hung a heavy-looking purse.

"The knights will first cross the 'river,'" Stentor said.

"Does he mean the ditch?" Kaye asked me. "It's not very wide. This doesn't seem very hard."

"I don't know. Maybe if the ditch is the river, the poles are supposed to be the Brown Castle? Keep listening," I answered.

Stentor started talking again. "Then the knights will run through the forest toward the castle," he cried as he pointed to the poles. I had been right about them.

"Kaye, that means the purses are the fair ladies!" I said, laughing.

"Sssh..." he said.

"The knights will climb the poles and rescue the fair ladies—although they will really be rescuing the purses that hold the prizes. The purse in the closest tower is filled with gold coins," cried Stentor.

"Pay attention, Kaye," Beau said. "Be sure to get to the first tower before Melchor."

Kaye nodded but didn't say anything.

Finally, Stentor held up an hourglass. "Do not forget the wolves are coming! If the knights have not reached the poles by the time the sand runs out, they may consider themselves eaten by wolves!"

The crowd loved that idea and they roared with laughter. They liked this contest, although I thought it was too easy. All Kaye had to do was jump over a ditch, run down the lists, and climb a pole. The pole even had pieces of wood attached to it like a ladder. Kaye and Melchor walked up to the edge of the ditch and waited to begin. Beau and I stayed behind.

I nudged Beau and asked him a question that was bothering me. "This seems too easy. Do you think the queen made this contest easy on purpose for Kaye?"

"I don't know," he answered. "I hope not. If it's easy for Kaye, it will be even easier for Melchor."

He was right. Melchor could cross that imaginary river with one big step. He probably wouldn't even have to climb the pole, but could just pull it down with his great big hairy arms.

"Oh, I don't have a very good feeling about this," I said to Beau. "Too bad he has to go out there by himself."

Just then Stentor yelled out one last thing, "All knights entering this contest must enter the contest accompanied by their squires."

"Looks like you get your wish, Reggie," Beau said. "You had better go with him."

"Me!" I cried. "I'm not a squire. I don't know how to be a knight's helper!"

Beau looked down at me from all his tallness. Sometimes I did not like being short.

He said very seriously, "Reggie, is Kaye a knight?"

"Yes," I said. I could see where this was going.

"Do you know how to help Kaye?" he asked.

"Yes," I said sulkily. "I am *always* helping Kaye."

"Then go out there with him and help him again. How hard is that?" he said.

"Fine. You win. I'm going," I said. I went out onto the lists. I was the last one there. The crowd cheered when they saw me stand next to Kaye. I liked that. I smiled and waved to them and lots of them waved back.

"Kaye," I said, "this might not be so bad. It seems easy."

Melchor overheard me. "It's easier than easy, little squire. You two had better run faster than rabbits, because you'll have to take three steps to match just one of mine. I'll have that prize from the first tower and the second tower too. Watch and see as I become The Knight's Knight," he bragged.

He shoved his young squire Michael behind him and hissed, "Stay out of the way, boy. The crowd wants to see me, not you."

Michael didn't say anything.

Stentor shouted out, "The Challenge of the Chivalrous Tales of Old will begin when you hear the trumpet blast!"

As we waited for the trumpeters, something didn't feel right.

"Kaye," I whispered, "they forgot part of the story. They have an imaginary river and wolves and forest and castle and lady, but they left out the vines and the sword at the bottom of the river. Do you think their story is different from mine?"

"Maybe," Kaye said slowly. "Maybe that part was too hard to put into the contest." He shrugged. "If that's true, it's too late for them to add the vines and the sword now. We'll just have to do what Stentor said."

"You mean what he bellowed!" I said, laughing.

Kaye started laughing too. Melchor glared at us, but Michael looked like he might like to know what the joke was. I felt bad for him. It couldn't be easy working for Melchor all the time.

The trumpets blared and Stentor turned the hourglass. Melchor took a big step and crossed the ditch. The rest of us had to back up and take a running leap to get across, but it still wasn't hard to do. Melchor raced down the lists toward the climbing poles.

Kaye was not far behind him. Michael and I were just behind Kaye. Poor Michael had a hard time trying to keep up with Melchor, and Melchor had completely forgotten about him.

Just then I heard a familiar twanging noise. It sounded like someone had shot an arrow. I quickly found out why. Some of the tournament helpers were crouched down low by the side of the field. One of them had shot an arrow straight across the lists in front of me and Michael. There was a light rope tied to that arrow and the tournament helpers pulled it tight at both ends. Michael and I both tripped over the rope at the same time and went facedown into the dirt.

Before I could jump up again, more tournament helpers appeared out of nowhere and put something cold around my ankle. I heard a locking noise. I was a prisoner, and so was Michael! The other ends of the chains locked around our ankles were attached to the walls at the sides of the lists, and they weren't very long chains. I couldn't go anywhere.

Suddenly I understood everything. The queen had not forgotten the vines.

"Kaye!" I cried out.

He looked back and saw what had happened to us. Then he looked at Melchor, who was far ahead of him.

"Kaye, the vines!" I yelled. "They didn't forget the vines!"

I saw Kaye look behind me, back toward the ditch. I looked back too, just in time to see one of the helpers throw the key to the lock on my ankle into the muddy, water-filled ditch.

I looked back at Kaye and his eyes met mine. I saw that he understood too.

"The sword!" he cried.

Stentor lifted the hourglass high in the air. It was already running low.

"The wolves!" cried the crowd. "Run, boy, run!" they yelled to Kaye.

He did run. But he ran the wrong way, back toward the ditch. When he reached it, he jumped right into the ditch and disappeared underwater. The crowd gasped.

I looked at the hourglass—time was running out. Melchor had reached the bottom of the first pole. There was no way that Kaye could win this now. He was still underwater. The crowd started yelling his name.

Suddenly he burst out of the water and took a few big breaths of air. He crawled out of the ditch and ran toward me. As he did so, he held the key up in the air, and the crowd started cheering.

But maybe they were cheering for Melchor, because he had reached the top of the first pole and was waving the prize purse in the air.

The sand in the hourglass was quickly disappearing as Kaye unlocked the shackles on my ankle.

"There's still time, Kaye," I said. "We can still make it to the second tower!"

He shook his head and ran over to set Michael free.

"Run! The wolves are coming!" screamed the crowd.

Michael left the field, but Kaye and I took off running toward the second pole. My lungs burned with dry fire, but we kept on going.

I looked up and saw Melchor climbing down the first pole with his prize purse clenched between his teeth, but we kept running anyway. When Melchor reached the ground, he ran to the second pole and started climbing to the top of that one too.

Then four things happened at once. Melchor reached the top of the second pole and waved the second purse for the crowd to see, Kaye and I touched the bottom of the second pole, and the last grain of sand fell through the hourglass. The trumpets blasted again, and Kaye and I looked at each other and knew we had lost.

Then Melchor climbed down the pole and started dancing around, waving both the prize purses in the air.

Part of the crowd was cheering and chanting "Melchor, Melchor, Melchor!"

Others in the crowd were cheering and yelling, "Sir Kaye and squire are safe from the wolves!"

Still others seemed upset and called out, "Boo," with angry faces.

I didn't know what was happening anymore.

Just then Stentor bellowed one word, "SILENCE!" and everyone froze.

CHApteR tHiRty

In the stillness that fell over the crowd, the queen rose from her seat in the middle of the grandstand and spoke to the crowds.

"Good people of Knox," she began, "today we have seen a remarkable contest. Two very different knights have competed in The Challenge of the Chivalrous Tales of Old, tales that are very dear to everyone in Knox. Although I am not from Knox, I too love these stories and hope that all of us can become as great as Sir Gregory in our own ways."

The crowd nodded its approval at her words and listened as she kept talking.

"Now I will come down and give the prize to the winner," she said.

She came down the stairs of the grandstand and entered the lists. Then she stepped onto Stentor's platform and the crowd cheered again, while she waved to both Kaye and Melchor so that they would join her.

"People of Knox," she began, "let us praise Sir Melchor, the winner of the prize, who climbed not one, but two towers, to rescue two 'fair maidens'! Indeed, Sir Melchor is a most worthy knight. His tremendous strength and bravery are beyond compare!"

The crowd cheered at this, but I could still hear some booing too.

The queen kept talking, "He has won both purses, and deservedly so. However, I am afraid, Sir Melchor, you will like the prize in the first purse better than the one in the second purse."

He smiled in a confused way and looked inside the first purse. He pulled out a handful of gold and waved it in the air. Some of the crowd cheered and some of them booed. When he opened the second purse, he sniffed at it and got an angry look on his face.

"Sweetmeats!" he cried. "What kind of prize is that?"

The queen laughed. "It is not much of a prize for you, Sir Melchor. It was meant for the boys."

He looked disgusted and threw the purse on the ground behind him. It landed at my feet. I picked it up and looked inside. Tourteletes—a whole bag of them! That *was* a good prize. Even I would climb a pole for tourteletes.

Now the crowd was confused. Some were laughing at the tourteletes, some were cheering for Melchor, and some were still booing.

"SILENCE!" roared Stentor. In an instant, it was so quiet you could have heard a leaf change from green to autumn red.

The queen drew Kaye forward. "Today, we must also honor Sir Kaye, who with no thought for himself or the prize, risked losing the contest to 'save' the lives of his friend and another boy. This was truly an act worthy of Sir Gregory and the tales of old. This was an act of chivalry and I hope that *all* the knights of Knox would do the same. Therefore I proclaim Sir Kaye to be The Knight's Knight and the winner of The Challenge of the Chivalrous Tales of Old!" The queen put a medal around Kaye's neck and then lifted his arm high in the air while the crowd broke into loud cheers with no booing at all.

"Hurrah for Sir Kaye, The Knight's Knight!" they cried over and over again.

The queen stepped back to talk to Stentor, and I saw Melchor's angry face. Kaye had won the praise and the title that Melchor had wanted. He was always going to hate Kaye now.

I ran up next to Kaye, just in time to hear Melchor hiss into Kaye's ear, "You had better watch out for me, boy! This isn't over!"

Then he disappeared into the crowds holding tightly to his purse full of gold.

Kaye looked at me. "It's never over, is it, Reggie?"

"I guess not," I said. "He reminds me of Charles. And they both smell worse than each other."

"Can't you ever be serious, Reggie?" Kaye asked, smiling.

"Yes, of course I can. *You're* the one who's always making jokes at the wrong times. But now's not the time to be serious. That whole crowd is cheering for *you*, because you beat big old Melchor by doing something he couldn't do. So wave your hands and smile at the crowd!" I told him.

Kaye laughed and did that and everybody cheered. And, as hard as it was to do it, I couldn't let Kaye be the only one being chivalrous that day. I opened up the prize purse Melchor had tossed aside and started throwing tourteletes out into the crowd. Now they were really cheering!

I saved two, though. One for Kaye and one for me. That was only fair.

On that last evening of the tournament, there was even more feasting and music and dancing than before. Kaye and Beau and I were right in the middle of it all. Kaye wore his medal and we ate and danced and ate again.

Everywhere we went, people cheered and called out, "Hurrah for Sir Kaye, The Knight's Knight!" Some of the little girls in the city threw flowers at us. I think they must have picked the flowers themselves, because they looked a lot like weeds to me.

One sleepy old man sitting outside of an inn stopped us and said to Kaye, "It did me good to see you out there today. That other knight was nothing more than a villain. You, young man, are a knight and a gentleman."

The man started snoring gently as his head nodded down to his chest. We started to tiptoe away, but he woke up again and said, "Maybe the queen knows what she's doing after all, Sir Kaye. See that you don't let her down."

"I won't," Kaye said. "I mean, I'll try not to."

But the man was asleep again.

The three of us walked back to the castle together. All around the castle, people were celebrating and having a good time, but the castle was the same as always.

"Look how dark and gloomy the castle is," I said.

"It's too bad," Beau said. "The castle should have all the best music and feasting and dancing after a tournament."

"Wait," Kaye said, grabbing my arm. "Look up there. There's a light!"

He was right. One of the windows showed a faint glow coming from deep within the room. It was the window of the queen's chambers.

Beau laughed. "Well, it's a beginning. Maybe someday it will be the whole castle that is clean and bright, instead of just our rooms."

"I think it will," Kaye said. "We can help make it happen."

"Beau," I said. "It is very strange to hear you say that only our rooms are clean. My mother always says exactly the opposite about my room at home."

chapter thirty-one

A week later, Kaye and I went home. Once again, Alfred went with us. It was comforting to have Old Stone Face there. After so much excitement at the tournament, it was pleasant to be with someone so dull.

As soon as we arrived at the Balfour estate, Meg came running out to meet us as though she were being chased by a wild boar.

"Kaye, Reggie, come quick!" Meg squealed. "Mum's really upset! Something terrible has happened!"

"Is it Father?" cried Kaye with a terrible twist in his voice. "Is he injured? What's happened?" Kaye raced up to the door of the hall just as Lady Martha came out.

"Oh, no, Kaye. The last time I heard from your father, he was doing well," said Lady Martha. "It's good to have you home," she continued, as she wrapped her arms tightly around him and pulled him close.

"It's nice to be home, Mum, but what's wrong?" Kaye asked again. At least I think that's what he asked. It was hard to hear him with his face crushed against his mum. His mum understood him though.

"It's Charles Atwood," said Lady Martha, letting go of Kaye. Her eyes were wet with tears.

I don't know if they were tears of happiness at seeing Kaye or tears of sadness about some horrible thing Charles had done. I think she had to be crying because of Charles. There was no reason to weep over Kaye. He was right there, safe and sound.

"What about Charles Atwood?" Kaye asked.

"He's been missing for almost two days now," said Lady Martha. "Charles' mother Eloise came here yesterday. She's terribly frightened because Charles went into the Knotted Woods and never came back. No one will help her find him, and she can't afford to pay the sheriff for his help, so she thought of you, Kaye."

"Of me?" Kaye asked, very surprised.

"She heard that you're a knight now," Lady Martha said, "and thought that you would help find him."

"I see," Kaye said slowly. "Very well then, we'll go look for him." He sighed a little bit. "I suppose we'd better start now while there's still plenty of daylight left."

"Be careful, Kaye," Lady Martha said. "You may be a knight, but you're still a boy. Charles may not just be lost. He may be held captive by bandits or he may have had an accident and been badly injured. Promise me that if you find something that is too much for you and Reggie to handle, you'll come back here for extra help. Promise me."

"Yes, Mum," he replied. "Of course I promise. I'm sure it will be all right. Reggie and I know these woods better than any other honest people around here. And we're good at sneaking through them without anyone noticing us. We're really the best ones to go."

Lady Martha's lips were pinched thin and tight, but she nodded. "I just wish you weren't the only ones willing to go. I wish your father was home." She put her hand on Kaye's shoulder and closed her eyes for a moment. When she opened them, she sounded tired. "Have you boys eaten lately?" she asked.

"No, Mum. It's been a few hours," Kaye replied. "I'm starving. And I'm sure Reggie could eat something." He grinned back at me.

I nodded. He was right. I was hungry enough to eat Alfred's leather shirt. But I wasn't hungry enough to forget what Kaye had just said we would do.

"Well, at least that's something I can help with," she continued. "I'll go pack something for you and Reggie to eat."

As soon as Lady Martha went inside, I pulled Kaye around to face me. "Have you lost your senses? Why would we go looking for Charles? Don't you remember what he said would happen if he saw us again?"

"I know, Reggie," Kaye said, "but I'm a knight now, and a knight's job is to help people who need help. Charles needs help right now."

"I know," I replied, "but you're talking about helping Charles Atwood!"

"Reggie," Kaye said, "I understand how you feel. You don't have to come with me if you don't want to."

I thought about this and looked at Old Stone Face, who was still waiting there, listening to everything. He stood as silent and unmovable as a rock. Only his long whiskers swayed gently in the breeze, and only his big red nose made him look human—or maybe it just made him look like a more colorful rock.

I heaved a big sigh. I wasn't going to get any help from Alfred. "I'll come along," I said.

Kaye's smile got a little bigger but I could tell that he was worried too.

Lady Martha came back outside and handed each of us two packages wrapped in coarse homespun cloth. They were warm to the touch.

"Put these meat pies in your saddlebags, boys. I packed a double helping for you, Reggie," she said. The rich scent of spiced meat filled my nose as I took the heavy parcels from her and tucked them safely away.

"Thank you, Lady Martha," I said.

"Yes, thank you, Mum," Kaye said. "We had better leave now."

We started off toward the Knotted Woods. At least we knew this part of the woods by heart.

"So, where should we look first?" I asked.

chapter thirty-two

"Let's check the hideout first," he said.

"You can't go there! If Charles sees you there," I asked, "won't he be angry?"

Kaye shrugged. "We'll have to take the risk and find out."

"Hmmph," I grunted. I could see why Alfred liked the word so much.

Kaye and I rode toward Charles' secret hideout and as we got closer, Kaye stopped. "Did you hear something, Reggie?" he asked.

I shook my head.

"Maybe we should leave the horses here for now and go quietly on foot," he suggested.

We moved softly toward the hideout, stopping every few yards to scan for danger, when we heard a faint voice cry out. "Hello, is someone there? I need help!"

"That sounds like Charles," I whispered. "He's in trouble. Do you think it's robbers?"

"No," Kaye said, "I don't think Charles would be calling for help if there were robbers with him. He must be alone. I'll try talking to him."

Kaye called out in a loud voice, "Charles, is that you?"

After a brief pause he answered, "Yes. Who are you?"

"First tell me what's happened. We're here to help," Kaye said.

"I'm stuck in a tree, and my leg is hurt," Charles said.

"How did you hurt your leg?" Kaye asked.

"A wolf was chasing me, and I hurt my leg trying to climb a tree," he answered.

"Where's the wolf now?" Kaye asked.

"He's still here." Charles said. "He's been waiting at the bottom of the tree for two days now. I've been talking to him, but I can't get down."

"Don't go anywhere, Charles, we'll think of something," Kaye said, with his usual bad joke at a bad time.

I groaned and thought I also heard a groan coming from Charles' direction. For the first time, I felt like he and I might have something in common. Then I remembered the wolf.

"How are we going to catch a wolf?" I asked.

"I don't know," Kaye said, putting his hand on his chin. A minute later Kaye raised his eyebrows and said, "I've got it. Reggie, can you find a long sturdy stick?"

"What are you going to use a stick for?" I asked.

"You'll see, Reggie, now please hurry!"

As I went to find a stick, Kaye pulled out his wool and knitting needles and went to work knitting a long cord, like he did when he rescued me from Martin's Bog.

When I found a good stick, Kaye made a sturdy noose from the knitted cord and attached it securely to the end of the stick. Then we crept toward Charles, keeping hidden. Once we were close enough to see him, we stopped to make our plan.

"Look at the wolf," Kaye whispered. "It looks like it hasn't eaten in months."

The young wolf had brown eyes and a cinnamon coat with gray and black streaks. Maybe it had lost its pack and hadn't been able to feed itself very well.

"Let's sneak around the clearing and get behind that big rock near the wolf. Then when I give the word, I'll get the noose around the wolf's neck and you help Charles out of the tree."

"Me!" I said, "Why do I have to help him out of the tree?"

"Fine!" Kaye said, "I'll help Charles out of the tree and you can get the noose over the wolf."

"Are those my only two choices?" I asked.

"It's one or the other," Kaye said, "so which one will it be?"

"Well," I said, "I guess I'll help Charles out of the tree. At least I know he won't eat me."

We slowly and silently worked our way behind the rock until we were close enough to spit on the wolf.

Then Kaye gave me the sign. Within one second, he had the noose around the wolf's neck and was holding on for dear life. I stared as the wolf struggled against the cord.

"Reggie! Get Charles out of the tree!" Kaye cried.

I looked up at Charles and I was surprised to see a helpless expression on his face. He was hungry and tired and hurt and didn't want to fight with me and Kaye anymore.

"Charles, do you think you can climb down the tree if I help you?" I asked.

"I'll try," Charles said.

I climbed part way up the tree as Charles slowly worked his way down. I tried to help him down the rest of the way, supporting his injured leg. By the time we reached the ground, Kaye had managed to get the wolf calmed down. Actually, the wolf was so hungry and tired that he was a lot like Charles. There was no fight left in him.

CHAPTER THIRTY-THREE

Two of the Knotted Woods' most dangerous creatures—the wolf and Charles Atwood—lay panting on the ground in front of us.

Kaye handed his water pouch to Charles. Charles looked up at Kaye, hesitated for a second, and then grabbed the water and started drinking. The wolf stared at us the whole time, like a loyal dog waiting for us to tell him what to do. He was a beautiful animal and he looked thirsty too.

"What about the wolf?" I asked. "He needs water too."

"You're right, Reggie," Kaye said. "What can we put the water in?"

Charles spoke in a husky voice. "I have a bowl."

"Perfect! Where is it?" I asked.

"It's in my secret hideout," Charles said, pointing to his beaver hut. "That's where I keep my things."

I knew exactly where to look, so I grabbed a crooked bowl and ran back to Kaye and Charles, yelling, "I found it!"

I got there just in time to hear Charles say, "The wolf's name is Mungo."

"You named the wolf?" Kaye asked.

"Yes," Charles said, "I just spent two days in a tree with no one else to talk to. I had to call him something besides Wolf."

"Well, he seems to like you," Kaye said.

I filled the bowl with water and carefully placed it in front of the wolf. He looked at the water and then back up at me and I could almost see a thank you coming from his eyes. He lapped up the water even faster than Charles had attacked Kaye's water pouch.

"You sure were thirsty, wolf!" I said.

"His name is Mungo," Charles said.

"Fine, his name is Mungo," I said. "I bet you're hungry too, aren't you Mungo?"

At mention of food, both Mungo's and Charles' ears perked up, so we opened the packets of meat pie and divided them among the four of us.

It looked like an eating contest between Charles and Mungo to see who would finish first, and I wasn't far behind. After we finished eating we sat there resting for a time. Then Charles broke the silence.

"Kaye, why did you come looking for me? I was always mean to you."

"Not always," Kaye said. "You needed help. Your mother was so worried about you. She's always been kind to me, and you're all she has."

"But I hated you," Charles said.

Kaye winced like he had bitten his tongue. "Why did you hate me?" he asked. "We used to be such good friends."

Charles stretched out on his back and looked up at the tree branches before answering. "It was because of my father.

He went away, but your father wouldn't even let you go away for training. He wanted you to stay together. Mine didn't."

"My father went away too," Kaye said.

"No," Charles said. "He had a reason. And he didn't want to go. It's different."

"You don't know that," Kaye said. "Your father was good to you before he left. Maybe he had a reason to go too. Maybe he didn't want to go either."

"Maybe," Charles said, "but I don't know."

We were so quiet for so long that a fox stepped into the clearing. When he saw Mungo, he stepped right back out again, but I knew him. It was the same fox that got me into all that trouble with quicksand in the first place. But the fox didn't know everything that had happened since then. I wasn't the same person, and that fox would have to think twice before fooling me again. I ran with wolves now—well, one wolf, anyway.

"We should probably be getting back," Kaye said finally.

"What about Mungo?" Charles said. "We can't just leave him."

"He's right," I said. "We can't leave him tied up by himself."

Kaye shook his head. "We can't take him with us either. No one's going to like it if we bring a wolf into the village."

"Then we'll have to bring him food and water, at least until Mungo gains some strength," I said.

"As soon as I can walk," Charles said, "I'll take care of him myself."

Kaye thought about this for a second. "Well, we'll have to be careful. After all, he's still a wolf. Charles, do you think you can ride on the back of my horse?"

"I think so," Charles said.

Kaye and I brought the horses back to Charles' hideout. They didn't like coming so close to Mungo, even though he was tied up. Kaye helped Charles stand up and carefully led him over to Kadar.

"Reggie," Kaye said, "help me get Charles up on Kadar."

I have trouble getting on my own horse without help, let alone shoving a boy twice my size over my shoulders onto a gigantic horse while trying not to hurt his injured leg. Then after all that was finished, we still had to do something about Mungo.

Kaye rode Kadar around the back side of the tree where the big rock was. I got onto my horse as Kaye climbed on top of the big rock so he was right above Mungo.

"Stand by, Reggie!" Kaye said, as he slipped the tip of his sword carefully under the noose around Mungo's neck. With a quick *thwip* of the sword, he cut the noose and set Mungo free.

Mungo looked up at Kaye with sad eyes. Kaye immediately got back onto Kadar.

"Sorry, Mungo," Kaye said, "but we have to go. We'll be back to bring you more food and water. Let's go, Reggie!"

We galloped off toward the village. I looked back and saw Mungo curl up under the tree, staring at us as we rode away.

It took longer than usual to get back. We had to stop and let Charles rest his leg several times, but we entered the village in the last glimmer of light from the setting sun. Eloise came running out to meet us. She was crying as she called out, "Charles, are you hurt? Where have you been?"

Some of the village boys were standing nearby and they looked shocked to see that Kaye had rescued Charles.

"Don't worry, Mum," Charles said, "I hurt my leg, but I'll be fine."

Kaye and I helped Charles off the horse and into the house.

"I'm so glad you're alive!" Eloise said. "I've been so worried about you. I thought you were gone for good. How did you hurt your leg?"

Kaye and I glanced at each and then Kaye said, "I think we'll leave you two alone. Reggie and I need to get back home."

"Oh, of course, Kaye," Eloise said, "I can't thank you boys enough for finding Charles. You two are truly heroes!"

I'd never seen Kaye smile more than he did at that moment. There was nothing he wanted more than to be a knight like his father. I liked being called a hero too. Maybe being chivalrous meant more than doing things you didn't want to do just because you had to. Sometimes being chivalrous meant making someone's life better.

"Thank you," Kaye said.

"Yes, thank you," I said too.

Lady Martha and Alfred were waiting for us in the courtyard when we arrived.

"Did you find Charles?" Lady Martha called out.

"Yes, Mum, he's at home. He hurt his leg, but he'll be fine."

"Kaye," said his mum, "I am so proud of you, and I know your father would be too. And I'm proud of you too, Reggie."

This was the second time in one day that I actually saw Kaye smile from ear to ear and this time I joined in. I glanced over at Old Stone Face, and for the first time he actually looked like he liked us as he nodded his head a few times in a row.

chapter thirty-four

I went home the next day and told my parents about all our adventures. They had heard about Kaye being knighted, but they wanted to know all the details. My father was speechless with joy when I told him that I was now good friends with the duke and the queen. He couldn't believe his good fortune in having a son that made such wonderful and powerful connections. I had a feeling I was safe from the monks for at least a little while.

During the next few weeks, Kaye and I took turns feeding Mungo until Charles could take care of him.

One day Kaye and I met to go riding, and when we returned to the castle, we saw a royal messenger leaving.

"I wonder what the message is about," Kaye said. "Maybe it's from Father." Kaye left Kadar in the courtyard and ran into the hall. I followed close behind him.

Kaye yelled out, "Mum! Is it from Father? Is it?"

"Calm down, Kaye," Lady Martha said. "There are two messages, one from your father and one from the queen. The queen wants you and Reggie to live at the castle and be company for Beau."

"But what about Father's message?" Kaye asked, completely ignoring the message from the queen.

"It's an unusual message," said Lady Martha, handing it to Kaye. "Here, you can read it for yourself—it's not good news for us."

"My dearest Martha, Meg, and Kaye, I miss you very much. I've heard from the queen about how she knighted you, my son, and how proud I should be of you. I *am* proud of you. You have acted like a knight should. I would like

so much to say I will be coming home to Knox soon but duty requires me to stay in Eldridge a while longer. There is something very strange happening here. I am afraid it means bad news for both countries. Maybe even war. I must try to discover the truth behind the strange events here before trouble begins. I hope to send you another message soon. Love, Henry."

"That's very mysterious," Kaye said, "I wonder what Father is investigating?"

We all thought hard for a moment, wondering what that strange message meant.

We never could have imagined that Sir Henry would uncover a wicked plot that would threaten the futures of both Knox and Eldridge, a conspiracy that had its roots deeply planted on both sides of the border.

In the meantime, Kaye and I made preparations to return to the castle. Within a few days, Alfred returned to take us back to Castle Forte where an adventure beyond imagination awaited us.

about the author

Don M. Winn is the award-winning author of eleven children's picture books, including *Superhero*; *The Higgledy-Piggledy Pigeon*; *Twitch the Squirrel and the Forbidden Bridge*; *Space Cop Zack, Protector of the Galaxy*; and *GARG's Secret Mission*.

Don has also written the *Sir Kaye the Boy Knight* series—an award-winning four-book series of chapter books for middle readers, which includes *The Knighting of Sir Kaye*, *The Lost Castle Treasure*, *Legend of the Forest Beast*, and *The Eldridge Conspiracy*.

Don currently lives with his family in Round Rock, Texas. Visit his website at **www.donwinn.com** for more information and all the latest news. If you liked this book, he'd love to hear from you.

You can e-mail him at **author@donwinn.com**.

Don't miss any of Kaye's adventures in the award-winning Sir Kaye the Boy Knight series!

Book 2: The Lost Castle Treasure

Can Kaye, Reggie, and Beau find a missing treasure in time to save the kingdom? Or will jealous knights succeed in their plot to make Kaye lose his knighthood forever?

❋ A Readers' Favorite Finalist ❋ A UK Wishing Shelf Awards Finalist
❋ A Foreword Reviews IndieFab Book of the Year Finalist

Book 3: Legend of the Forest Beast

Kaye, Reggie, and Beau must capture a shipment of valuable gems before it leaves the country to prevent a rebel knight from funding a war against Knox.

❋ A Moonbeam Children's Book Award Silver Winner
❋ A UK Wishing Shelf Awards Finalist

Book 4: The Eldridge Conspiracy

The final book in the Sir Kaye series. Kaye enters Eldridge alone to seek the only man who can tell him how to save his father's life.

❋ A Readers' Favorite Bronze Medal Winner
❋ A Mom's Choice Award Gold Medal Recipient

CPSIA information can be obtained
at www.ICGtesting.com
Printed in the USA
FFOW03n1904040318
45351732-46018FF